Other Books by R.Y. Suben

The Dreamers — Noora's Quest

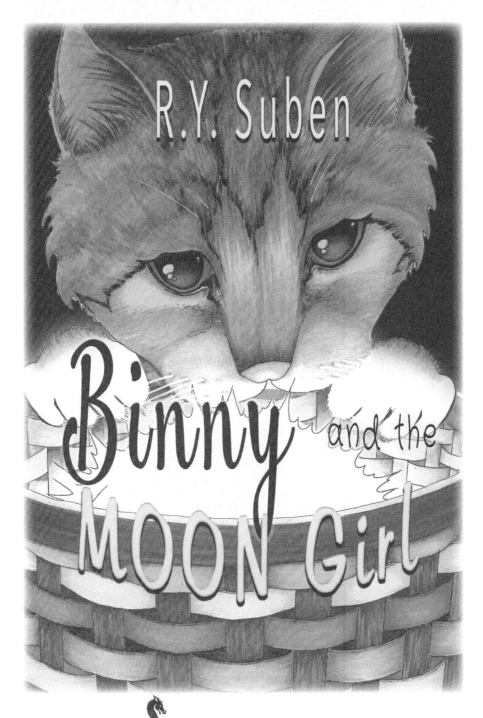

R.Y. Suben

Binny and the MOON Girl

A Dragonfeather Book

Bedazzled Ink Publishing Company * Fairfield, California

978-1-949290-83-7 paperback

Cover art
by
Trish Ellis

Cover Design
by

Sapling
Studio

Dragonfeather Books
a division of
Bedazzled Ink Publishing Company
Fairfield, California
http://www.bedazzledink.com

I'm a limping cat
With a crooked tail
I can't walk straight.

My distinct fluttering purrs chime like a bell
in harmony with my superior sense of smell.
I'm unique in every sense—

I'm curious, a gifted cat.
Mastered your tongue.
I stand to protect
with sprits of kindliness.

I'm Binny, a splendid tabby cat.

For my children and my adorable cats.

Chapter 1

"RUNNING LATE TO my meeting, dear. See you later," Binny meowed in excitement to Mrs. Cobbler and disappeared out through her private pet door into the dark.

She and Mrs. Cobbler were residents of Nauvoo, a picturesque, quiet, historical town in central Illinois. The name meant "pleasant land" or "beautiful place" in Hebrew, and the pretty hamlet rested on the banks of the Mississippi River across from Fort Madison, Iowa. Binny and Mrs. Cobbler lived in a two-story cedar house on Ripley Street, close to the Nauvoo State Park—convenient for afternoon walks, but still close to local stores for shopping.

Binny took the same path she always did as she headed toward the state park to meet the members of Friendly Pets, Chapter 9. Staying on top of the neighborhood news took priority and was a bright part of her life. There had been many home break-ins in town that week, making all the brothers and sisters in her club anxious. Binny was worried as well. And since that evening's meeting was about preventing more break-ins, she didn't want to miss it.

The full moon glowed on her path between the shadows of trees, and a balmy breeze brought the fragrant smell of spring flowers. Binny hastily continued on her way, thinking about starting a new neighborhood watch program. She stepped into a small hole. Her four paws sank into a strange, squishy substance, and Binny winced at the smell and tapped one of her paws against it. She dragged herself from the hole and sniffed her forepaws. *Could it be spilled paint?* she wondered. Her vertical pupils and retinal receptors opened up to inspect the strange, red residue. It didn't look like paint. Was it blood? Human or animal blood?

Binny raised her right leg and gingerly licked her paw. It tasted salty and smelled utterly unfamiliar.

Perhaps it didn't belong to this World. She shivered with that thought and walked farther away from the puddle. The cold breeze touched her spine, running through her body to her raised tail. Carefully, she checked the walking path ahead and spotted odd, reddish clusters along the way in the moonlight.

Binny hesitated, but her curiosity to follow won against her desire to go to the meeting. She had a hunch extraordinary things were about to happen and decided to follow the randomly spread grains while making herself familiar with their odd smell. Her mind was entirely focused on this new mission. *I must see what these lead to!* she thought, setting off. And then, at the end of the trail, by the left side, under the oak tree, was a *thing*.

"It came from the sky, perhaps from the moon," a voice said from overhead, and Binny looked up to see the enormous eyes of Adel, the screech owl, peering down at her. "The thing cries and shines nonstop."

Eyes wide, Binny stood for a second and stared at the thing, trying to grasp its shape. It looked like a glowing ball, but it was noisy. *I have never seen a gleaming, crying ball.* Her curiosity won again, and she approached the thing.

"Don't get any closer! It might be harmful!" Adel screeched, hopping between branches. "Who, *whoo*! Who, *whooo* knows what it might do to you?"

Adel's screech echoed in the breeze, which made the thing's sobs grow louder.

"Don't worry, Adel. Calm down," Binny meowed.

Adel rounded his wings, raised his pointed ear tufts, and tried to camouflage himself as tree bark. His yellow eyes aimed at the thing like flashlights piercing in the night. He hooted one more time to warn Binny.

"It's just a glowing ball, Adel." Intrigued by the thing's heartbreaking moans, Binny cautiously touched it with her left paw and brushed its thick, sticky skin. Staring at its odd, tangled, arm-like tassels in astonishment, she asked, "Hi, there. Who are you? Where do you come from?"

The thing's glow brightened, and Adel fled to another tree, screeching, "Run, Binny! Run! It will explode!"

The thing only wept harder.

Binny felt dazed by its gleaming light. "It seems harmless, Adel. It just seems to need our help."

Adel turned his head back and forth. "Not from me. This is all you, Binny."

Binny sighed, rolled her eyes at Adel, and turned back to the thing, trying to make her voice as soothing as possible. "Hey, glowing ball thing, relax a bit. I want to help you."

Binny's voice seemed to soothe the thing. She softly touched its skin and asked, "Come stay at my home and warm up tonight?" Without waiting for its reply, Binny grabbed it gently in her jaws and walked back to Mrs. Cobbler's house, forgetting about her important club meeting.

To avoid the busy streets, she took the shortcut toward the north. It took all her strength to carry the thing; it was heavy, and every time it squirmed, it dragged Binny down. Before long, every muscle from her jaws to her legs buckled. Overwhelmed, she set the thing down and looked around, giving herself a moment to breathe.

Binny gingerly gripped the ball once more with her teeth and went on. She scurried onward, avoiding the streetlights, creeping through ditches and around hedges. When she finally spotted the glistening silhouette of the Lutheran church in the darkness, she relaxed. She was almost home.

Chapter 2

"IS THAT YOU, Binny? You are early, dear," Mrs. Cobbler called from the kitchen.

Mary Cobbler was a retired elementary school teacher. She had moved to Nauvoo forty years ago after marrying her husband, Tom. Their home had been spectacular, spotless, and well-maintained. Happiness had always sparkled on their faces, and heartwarming waves of laughter had resonated in their house. That was until Mr. Cobbler—a retired high school math teacher, skillful handyman, and loving husband—passed away from a massive heart attack eight years earlier.

Mrs. Cobbler aged beyond her years after that day. Her hair turned gray much faster shortly after the funeral, and the creases in her face grew deep from mourning. Since that day, it had just been the two of them: Binny and Mrs. Cobbler.

Binny gently set the glowing ball in the shoe closet and nudged the door so that it was only open a crack. "Please be quiet," she whispered to the thing. "I'll come back. And for your own sake, get your glowing under control," she added before going to greet Mrs. Cobbler.

"How was your night out, sweetie?" Mrs. Cobbler asked, smiling as she ambled into the foyer. Binny had become the center of Mrs. Cobbler's attention, as if she were her baby.

But before Binny could respond to the question, a watery moan came from the shoe closet.

Mrs. Cobbler's face turned pale, and she stepped back, peering in the direction of the sound. "Who is there?"

Binny ran to the shoe closet and hissed at the thing to stop crying. Then she gave assuring meows to Mrs. Cobbler that nothing was there.

Mrs. Cobbler picked Binny up, gave her a warm hug, and stroked her smoky striped forehead. "Oh, dear, it might be a mouse. I should call pest control tomorrow."

Binny inhaled the calming chamomile and honey fragrance as her mistress's short silver hair brushed across her face. In return, she licked Mrs. Cobbler's saggy chin—her way of saying, *I adore you.*

Mrs. Cobbler set Binny down on the wood floor and turned toward the living room. The old wood creaked as she shuffled over to her favorite chair by the fireplace.

Much like the loss of her husband had aged Mrs. Cobbler, the house they had shared deteriorated with her. The faucets dripped, and air in the pipes gurgled and echoed in the walls. Door hinges had grown rusty and squeaked when they were opened and shut. The windows whistled and creaked in the wind. And the two maestros of this awkward orchestra were the groaning heater in the winter and the buzzing air conditioner in the summer.

Binny would endure all manner of annoying noises if she could hear the sweet sound of Mrs. Cobbler's laughter and enchanting songs again. She missed those, most of all. Nowadays, the only sound from Mrs. Cobbler was the defeated moan of forgetfulness. Misplacing things around the house had become a significant problem. She had once lost her car keys and could not drive for two days. Luckily, Binny found them before they ran out of food.

Binny plodded toward Mrs. Cobbler and rubbed up against her legs to tell her, *You are the sweetest lady I have ever known.* Then she rolled on the floor and wiggled for attention, and Mrs. Cobbler gave a weak but loving smile in return. Binny gazed sadly into Mrs. Cobbler's tired face. Behind it, there was a Good Samaritan, a compassionate woman, who always gave help to whoever needed it. Binny bounced onto Mrs. Cobbler's lap and nuzzled her face.

When Binny was a three-month-old kitten, eagerly trying to cross the street, her mom, Belle, had been hit by a car while running after her; she had died instantly. If Mrs. Cobbler hadn't taken Binny to the hospital right away, she would be resting underground next to her mother. After many painful operations, Binny had recovered from her wounds. Mrs. Cobbler gave her a cozy and happy home, cuddled with her, and cheered her up, making it possible for Binny to forget that she was an orphan.

When she was a year old, Binny realized that due to her accident, she was unique: Her rear right leg was shorter than her left one. She managed to camouflage her limping by taking slow steps with frequent stops. But it was impossible to hide her short, broken tail that barely stayed up all the way. *I'm not an attractive cat, but I'm the most loving cat with an extraordinary sense of smell,* she told herself. She had found a way of discovering the best reasons to love herself and for others to accept and love her, too.

Her memories were interrupted by Mrs. Cobbler gently saying, "Goodnight, Binny. Sleep tight, my baby."

She softly meowed, "Same to you."

Binny shivered, thinking what might happen if Mrs. Cobbler spotted the thing in the closet. The sudden sight of it could be harmful to her weak heart. How was she going to keep it a secret?

Chapter 3

BINNY RAISED HER ears and waited, listening to Mrs. Cobbler's steps echoing on the squeaky stairs.

After hearing the bedroom door shut, she tiptoed to the shoe closet and whispered, "Now, shush. Don't glow or make a sound. I'll take you to the guest room."

Binny gently gripped the thing with her teeth and then quietly climbed the stairs, hoping that Mrs. Cobbler would be deep asleep already. Nudging the partially ajar guest room door open was easy; hiding the thing would be a challenge, though. Then Binny flinched, remembering Mrs. Cobbler's niece, Ariel, would be visiting during spring break.

Binny adored Mrs. Cobbler's youngest niece, despite getting off to a rocky start. A fair-skinned girl with reddish-brown hair and freckles sprinkled across her cheeks, Ariel had been an annoying toddler when she first showed up with her mom, Emily, at Mr. Cobbler's funeral. Ariel did what toddlers usually do and chased Binny until her bedtime; Binny ran away from her as much as she could and felt sorry for not grieving properly for Mr. Cobbler's death. Since then, Ariel has visited Mrs. Cobbler every spring break and summer vacation.

When Ariel was four years old, her cheeks had swelled, giving her a chipmunk-like appearance. Her mom and dad, both nurses at the Peoria urgent care center, told Mrs. Cobbler that Ariel was experiencing something similar to mumps, even though she had been vaccinated for it. It had been a strange case. She had a high fever, runny nose, and red, watery eyes for more than three weeks. While Mrs. Cobbler and Binny were visiting Ariel at the hospital, the girl had what the doctor called a mild seizure. And it was that incident, Binny decided, that had changed Ariel—something magical had happened to her during the seizure.

Ariel was able to understand animal speech.

Binny made this discovery shortly after the girl's recovery when Ariel came for summer break. Binny leaped into her arms and licked her face, meowing, "I missed you."

Ariel whispered back, "I missed you too, Binny."

Binny's ears swiveled upright in surprise. *Did she understand me?* she thought, eyes wide, but then she realized what must have happened. *She could tell I was saying I missed her because of the way I jumped to her and kissed her.*

Binny thought nothing was unusual until dinner, when Ariel didn't want to drink her glass of milk.

"Drink your milk. It's good for you, Ariel," Binny meowed.

"I'm full, Binny," Ariel said with a huff.

Binny twitched her ears again, curled her crooked tail, and was alongside Ariel in one leap. "Did you understand what I said?" she asked, realizing how crazy it sounded.

Ariel chuckled. "Yes, my dear. I realized I could understand animals after I got home from the hospital—my friend brought her cat, Sammi, over for a visit."

Ever since that day, Binny had looked forward to Ariel's school vacation visits all the more. Sending Ariel to Auntie's house for long holidays worked well for Ariel's parents, and Mrs. Cobbler and Ariel both looked forward to those spring and summer break days.

Ariel was twelve now, completing sixth grade at Union Junior High, and she had recently stopped going to after-school care. Binny knew she was thrilled; Ariel was proud of becoming more independent. Ariel told Binny that her mom, Emily, meticulously planned her after-school activities, a to-do list to complete alongside her homework, like emptying the dishwasher and organizing her room. But Ariel still had plenty of time to text, read Nancy Drew stories, or play Minecraft on her Xbox.

When Binny asked Ariel how her studies were going, she smiled. "No worries, Binny. My parents check my homework. Besides, I'm okay with staying home alone, even for the one-off days like parent-teacher conferences or Martin Luther King Day. I didn't like going to the YMCA and being surrounded by noisy kids I hardly knew. I wish my parents would drive me to Auntie Cobbler's house, instead, so I could play with you. But it's a two-hour drive from home, too far for a day trip."

But now that Binny had chosen to keep the strange creature, her head spun with thoughts and worries about Ariel finding it. Her eyes darted back and forth, and she whirled around in circles. She tried to control her nervous circling and focused on looking for a safer place to hide her guest. A practical solution was to put the thing under the bed. But what would happen if Ariel decided to vacuum under there? Binny could picture the scene: She would run from the house, never to return, screaming about a monster under her bed. The safer option would be the closet . . . if she could open it.

Binny put the thing down under the nightstand and then jumped, aiming for the closet's doorknob. No luck. After a few tries, she quickly tired, and the thing that looked like a ball whimpered and glowed.

"Shush! Please don't wake up Mrs. Cobbler," Binny hissed.

The thing only glowed brighter and groaned. Feeling helpless to calm this blasted ball, Binny started to panic. *What if this is like some sort of grenade I've let in, ready to detonate at any second?* She was a dauntless cat, and she didn't mind facing the consequences. *But I should have thought twice about endangering my guardian's safety and reputation.*

Binny imagined the newspaper headlines, TV cameras, and loud reporters waiting on their doorstep, asking endless questions about hiding a strange, explosive creature. What would happen if the authorities found Binny had hidden this bizarre object in the house? Was it a crime to hide valuable evidence about alien life?

She sighed, escaping from her nightmarish thoughts, and told herself, *Stop panicking. I can handle this.*

Binny stretched her front legs, twitched her body, and then prowled toward the thing, which whimpered and glowed as she drew near.

"This place is safe for you, but only if you stop all the crying and glowing," Binny said forcefully. "Put yourself in order and tell me who you are."

Her commanding voice seemed to work; the thing settled and quieted. Binny brushed its wrinkly skin with her right paw and breathed in its tangy odor. Her touch must have reached a ticklish spot because the thing giggled, and Binny couldn't help but smile. It was becoming obvious to Binny that this creature communicated by glowing. *Perhaps it was using an alphabet similar to Morse code.*

Binny's retinal receptors scanned the ball, taking in its not-perfectly-round shape, its faint tan color, and reddish grains peeking out from inside. It sort of deflated and whooshed under her paw.

She had a thought, and asked, "Hey, are you hungry?"

She sprinted to the kitchen to get some of her food, thinking that building trust was a must before asking questions. She returned and set down bits of kibble by the knotted, tassel-like strands and stayed still, watching curiously. After only a moment, the thing twisted and rolled over onto the cluster of kibbles and made crunching sounds. When it finished, it giggled and glowed.

Binny cringed away from the smell of reddish spills from the thing. She kept her manners intact.

"Now, we're talking. I'll bring more food and some water"

After several back-and-forth trips to Mrs. Cobbler's kitchen, Binny decided that the situation was under her control. The time was right to ask questions, and she should start with the simple ones.

"So . . . where do you come from?"

The thing didn't respond.

"Okay. We can sort that out later. Can you at least tell me if you are a boy or a girl? Glow twice for girl, once for boy."

The thing glowed twice, giggled, and hummed.

"Oh—good! I'll call you—" Binny thought hard for a moment, gazing at the glowing orb, and then smiled. "I'll call you Moon Girl."

Proud of her accomplishment, Binny curled closer to her guest. She purred joyfully about her discovery and soon fell asleep.

In the middle of the night, Binny woke yowling from a nightmare. The noise echoed in her upright ears. She arched her back, her fur bristling, and tried to remember her terrible dream, wondering if perhaps she was more distraught about deceiving Ariel than she thought.

Binny waggled her crooked tail with frustration and tried to justify hiding the odd creature. *No, it wasn't a betrayal,* Binny decided. *It was a noble intention to help her survive.*

But in the back of her mind, Binny wondered how long she could keep Moon Girl a secret from the ones she loved.

Chapter 4

"BINNY, WE NEED to see Dr. Andreas," Mrs. Cobbler said. "I have filled your plate four times a day this week. You are eating much more than usual, but you aren't gaining weight. I'm worried about you."

Binny was sitting on Mrs. Cobbler's lap, preparing to take her usual afternoon nap. She lifted her ears, fully awakened by the threat of a doctor's appointment. She was angry at herself for being careless and decided from then on, she would feed Moon Girl directly from the bag of kibble instead of her plate.

Binny sprang into the air and rolled over on the old Persian carpet. Then she ran to the corner of the room and grabbed her softball, trying to look as perky and energetic as possible as she trotted over and dropped it at Mrs. Cobbler's feet.

Mrs. Cobbler walked to the kitchen to re-fill Binny's plate, saying, "Oh, baby. I'm sure you're fine, but let's make sure."

Binny wished for a miracle, some sort of distraction to make Mrs. Cobbler forget calling Dr. Andreas. And just then, the doorbell rang, granting Binny's wish. Jenn, Mrs. Cobbler's close friend, was stopping by to bring over her favorite yellow roses. Jenn was a retired English teacher and had lived her entire life in Nauvoo. She had been Mrs. Cobbler's close friend since high school, and they were always telling each other, *born in Nauvoo, stuck in Nauvoo.*

Binny breathed a sigh of relief. Visiting Dr. Andreas's office was no longer a great threat . . . but the most significant danger was Ariel and her fast-approaching visit. If Ariel found Moon Girl, she might tell Mrs. Cobbler. It wouldn't be safe to keep Moon Girl under the nightstand during her stay; Binny knew she would have to move Moon Girl to a safer place, and soon. *I couldn't open the closet, and besides, it really isn't a secure place, either.* She knew that as soon as the curious girl walked through the front door, she would start ruling the house as hers.

Binny decided to call an urgent neighborhood meeting to ask for help from her club members. At this time of the year, she would be relaxing in the sun, doing nothing—but those lazy days were over. Now, she had responsibility for Moon Girl's well-being. She stepped out to the front porch, breathed the fragrant spring air into her lungs, and meandered toward the magnolia tree at the far corner of the house.

"Meow, Miss Polly," she called to the friendly cardinal, a longtime resident of the magnolia tree.

"It has been such a long time since I've heard from you, my lady," Polly chirped. "To what do I owe this pleasure?"

"I need to call an emergency meeting tonight, at the state park, at eight o'clock. Could you spread the word?"

Polly readily agreed and flew off.

Before the meeting that night, Binny brought Moon Girl her food. She watched her devour the kibble, all the while glowing with joy. Binny purred softly and twitched her whiskers as Moon Girl rolled over next to her. She then giggled and returned to her hiding spot beneath the nightstand leaving a trial of reddish musty grains. Binny ignored the scent and swept them with her front paws under the bed, thinking that she must get used to Moon Girl's discharge.

Binny entertained the thought of taking Moon Girl as her own baby. She always dreamed of becoming a mother, but because of the horrible accident from when she was a kitten, bearing a child was impossible. Binny wasn't only a limping cat with a short tail, she was also an infertile cat who had a burning desire to become a mother. Now, she felt as though she had a chance for that with Moon Girl. She could experience the instincts she thought she'd never use.

But . . . how can I do that without knowing how to care for Moon Girl? She waited a tail's length of time, pondering this sudden, strong bond to this odd, helpless, and yet adorable creature. She gazed at Moon Girl and sang, "Sleep tight and sleep well, my girl. The night will be your blanket, keeping you warm. The stars will illuminate your dreams. Happy dreams until a new morning."

"Mom will be away for a short time. Please be quiet to keep yourself safe." Feeling a thrill of excitement when she spoke the word *mom*, Binny trembled with racing thoughts, suddenly much more afraid of losing Moon Girl.

Their meeting place was in the most secluded northeast side of the park, close by Horton Lake, and it took no longer than ten tail lengths to get there. She padded along slowly, listening to the crickets' chorus. Her fur prickled as the chill air brushed over her body.

When Binny got to the meeting spot, she was surprised at the great turnout, despite the short notice.

The seven board members sat on the higher ground; others sat by their ranks and the number of years in service to the Friendly Pets, Chapter 9 club. The board president, Chance, was a lustrous golden retriever. He was a very kind, friendly, and intelligent dog who'd held the board administrator position for many years. He was athletic and well-known for his superb swimming skills. Chance opened the meeting, asking Binny about her emergency agenda.

Binny took a deep breath, knowing her speech must be brief but convincing. She pointed to Adel. "Our night watcher, Adel, found a glowing, crying ball."

The members of the club all chattered and shouted at once.

Binny held up a paw, asking for silence, and after a moment, the group settled. "Adel, could you tell us where this strange thing came from?"

Adel screeched, "Whoo! The thing came from the sky, crying and glowing, glowing and crying. I warned you, Binny."

The pets all shouted out questions.

"The thing?"

"What is it?"

"Where is it now?"

"She needed my help, Adel," Binny replied with a calm voice. "I brought her home and hid her behind a nightstand in the guest room. She's harmless and cuter than anything you have ever seen. I'm here today asking for your help to move her to a safer place. Ariel, Mrs. Cobbler's niece, is coming for spring break, so the guest room wouldn't be secure for my Moon Girl."

"Moon Girl?"

"Is that what you call it?"

"Does it talk?"

"I told you," Adel said with a huffing hoot. "It is a glowing ball, and it cries nonstop."

Binny shook her head. "Not anymore, Adel. She laughs and giggles, now. I think she talks using light—some form of code, maybe. I know it seems weird, but if you see her with your own eyes," she turned to the club members, "you'll find her fabulous. I love her very much."

"I can help you to move your girl to a safer place. Do you have a plan?" Cleo, Dr. Andreas' German shepherd, asked as she came forward. She was a large dog, with a black mask and saddle over a long, tan coat. All the club members respected Cleo's intelligence, speed, strength, and keen sense of smell. She raised her long neck, straightened her large ears, and swung her bushy tail, looking at each pet in turn. "Anyone else?"

"Come on, now guys. Step up," Chance called out, breaking the silence.

Leonard, a pug, waddled forward. "We're dealing with a bizarre creature. It might be the beginning of an alien invasion. Helping this thing is a threat to our society. We must report it to the authorities."

A loud wave of fearful grumbling and mutterings rose up from the gathered members.

"Please, speak to the meeting floor," Chance called, trying to restore order.

"Don't you trust Binny?" Cleo asked. "She says Moon Girl is harmless."

Binny nodded vigorously. "Moon Girl is *not* a part of an alien invasion. She is a cute and harmless creature."

"I suggest we vote for helping Binny," Cleo said to the group.

Missy, Jenn's Siamese cat, gave her silver-gray fur a shake. "I second the motion."

After voting, Chance announced a narrow margin victory to help Moon Girl. "Now, it is our responsibility to find a safer place to hide Binny's girl. Any suggestions?"

Chapter 5

"HOW ABOUT MY backyard summer house?" Missy suggested, wiggling her long, sleek tail.

Binny paced and nervously pawed at the grass. "That won't work, Missy. Your home is too far from mine. It would be hard for me to take care of her there."

There were many ideas, but none were practical to keep Moon Girl close to Binny.

Binny shook her head in dismay. "Let's adjourn the meeting for tonight, Chance."

Chance scratched a spot behind his ear, thinking hard. "Binny," he said after a moment. "How about your basement? Would Mrs. Cobbler or Ariel go down there?"

Binny walked back and forth, thinking, and then shook her head. "But I can't open the basement door."

Chance thoughtfully scratched his ear again. "How about through the basement window, from outside? I can set up an investigation team to find a way to get you into that basement."

"Great idea," Binny said, feeling hopeful—but then her heart sank. "But Ariel is coming tomorrow afternoon—how will I distract Mrs. Cobbler so that I can move Moon Girl?"

"I can divert Mrs. Cobbler's attention," Missy volunteered, nodding. "I'm very talkative and much more charming than any of the other club members. Mrs. Cobbler adores me."

Cleo came forward and raised her right paw. "I will find a way to enter the basement. Polly can patrol the front yard while Chance and I break into the basement."

Chance stood in front of the attendees. "It is almost midnight. We have a plan to execute. Meeting adjourned!" he howled.

On the way home, Binny felt genuinely blessed to have such good friends. She paced furiously all night.

The next morning, Missy was at Mrs. Cobbler's door with her irresistible meowing and quickly ended up on the old lady's lap. Polly, the cardinal, was perched on top of the magnolia tree, ready to sound the alert.

Chance carefully inspected the basement window. "I'll try to push the frame from the left. You try the right side."

Cleo approached the window and sniffed the rotten frame. They both pushed the edges as hard as they could with their front paws, but nothing happened.

Cleo scrutinized the frame. "We don't need to destroy it. We just need to make an opening wide enough for Binny and her girl," she whispered.

"See those large cracks?" Chance pointed with his snout. "That is where the wood is weakest. Let's push hard from the corners."

On their second try, Polly desperately flapped her wings. "Ariel is here with her mom!"

"She's early," Chance said.

"We still have time before they reach the front door," Cleo growled. "Chance, let's push harder." She turned to the panicking bird. "Polly, distract them."

They shoved hard again with their all strength, but it didn't budge.

"Cleo, how about we regroup and recruit someone who can hammer and drill?" Chance said.

Cleo paused, her head tilted. "Alice? The exotic woodpecker?"

Chance shrugged. "Worth a shot."

"But her racket will get the attention of the whole house," Cleo said, already shaking her head.

"Our team could help out with that," Chance offered. "It's all we've got. Let's just hope Binny agrees to our plan."

They padded to the front porch, dropping their gaze to the ground with shame as Binny and Mrs. Cobbler, still holding

Missy, came out the front door. Ariel ran and hugged her aunt, then Binny. She smiled at Chance and Cleo, not noticing their unhappy faces. "What a pleasant surprise. Thank you for coming."

Binny saw her friends' downcast eyes and lowered tails. "It didn't work, huh?" she whispered as Ariel chattered away to Mrs. Cobbler.

"We have one more option," Chance muttered. "We're going to ask for Alice's help, with the rest of the team creating a distraction. What do you think?"

"Do I have a choice?" Binny sighed. "Ok. Let's see the exotic woodpecker, Chance."

Missy jumped down from Mrs. Cobbler's arms. With a sad head shake and her tail tucked behind her left leg, she yowled at Binny, "Next time!"

Chance swished his tail, looking down at Binny. "You must come to help us convince Alice."

Lunchtime was a golden opportunity for Binny to slip from the house while the family caught up around the table. She scurried toward Chance, waiting for her in the front yard. "Have you been here a long time?"

"Not at all. I'm all yours, my lady," Chance said with a chuckle.

"I don't have much time. I don't want Ariel to notice I'm out," she said, looking over her shoulder with worry.

Chance took the lead toward Park Street, mostly quiet at this time of the day. The sun soon penetrated their fur, and sweat coated their bodies, dragging them toward the ground. Chance slowed a bit for Binny to catch up.

Binny shook her prickly pellet. "I'm fine, Chance. No worries."

It was easy to find Alice. Her home by Horton Lake was a manmade fishing dam, and the pets often wondered why Alice chose to live near fishing grounds so close to a trailer park; there were more secluded places with tall trees by the river. They had decided as a group that only an exotic bird would do that.

When Chance greeted Alice and asked for her help, she shook her head. "No way! Can't you see? I'm swamped." She made her point final with a swift jab of her pointy beak and an irritated flick of her wings.

"Please, miss. It's a life or death situation," Chance pleaded.

Binny groaned. "Total exotic," she added with a low yowl.

Chance leaned his front paws on the trunk. "Do you know anyone else who can help us, miss?"

"Try the Red-Capped couple. Polly can tell you where they are." Alice clung to the old tree trunk and hammered the old oak branch with her sharp beak.

Binny couldn't hide her disappointment. Her whiskers drooped no matter how Chance tried to cheer her up.

"We haven't talked to the Red-Capped couple, yet. Clear your dark thoughts, Binny," Chance insisted.

Binny winced. "It just seems so farfetched. I need to go—and I pray that Ariel hasn't discovered I'm away from the house." She scampered toward the porch as Chance bounded to the magnolia tree, and she paused to listen to the exchange.

"Polly, Alice refused to help. Could you ask the Red-Capped woodpeckers if they are willing to help to hammer and drill?"

Polly was excited about her new assignment. Proud of supporting her community, she chirped in excitement. "Good choice. Mr. and Mrs. Hammers live on the maple tree by the river. They love to drill old homes for insects. Surely, they can help us." She flapped her wings in excitement, and then flew toward the edge of town along the Mississippi River to talk to the Red-Capped couple.

The sun was setting, and the chilly air was settling in. Polly flew through a swaying mixture of green and red, and the air under her wings filled her lungs with a balmy earthiness. She looked over the oak and maple trees lining the north fork of the calmly flowing Mississippi River as it met the western branch on the edge of the town, erasing the memories of its tributaries that had overflowed in the heavy rain season, closing roads and bridges.

Polly descended slowly to the maple tree where the woodpecker pair lived, announcing her presence loudly, knowing that was the only way to get noticed over their constant drumming.

"Hello? Mr. and Mrs. Hammers?" Polly called out multiple times.

"Oh, hello, Polly. What is it, dear?" Mrs. Hammers chirped.

"We need your assistance for Binny, Mrs. Hammers."

Along with the tempting offer of a colony of worms nesting in the rotten wood frame that Cleo had mentioned, Polly told Mr. and Mrs. Hammer the story of Moon Girl.

"Certainly, we'll help!" they shrilled. "We should give a hand to one another in hard times."

Polly and Binny needed to figure out a diversion, to cover up the noise that Mr. and Mrs. Hammer would make. Binny suddenly thought of the choir, but that would mean they couldn't co-ordinate everything to happen until the morning because they would have to round up all the members of the choir.

"Oh no," thought Binny, "I'll have to keep hiding Moon Girl over night!" But there was nothing else that could be done.

Polly agreed with Binny's idea, and explained the plan to the Hammers. They agreed, and then continued on with their loud rat-a-tat-tat against the rotten branch they were working on.

Not only did the Hammers agree to help, but Chapter 9's choir gladly accepted Cleo's invitation to show up at Mrs. Cobbler's door early the next morning. Even though the choir had only been recently established, they had become well known in a short time. The members included a baritone basset hound, a tenor Maltese, a soprano Balinese, a mezzo-soprano Chantilly-Tiffany cat, and two altos Red-Breasted robins. Binny told them Mrs. Cobbler would be busy cooking her famous blueberry pancakes for Ariel, which would be the perfect time for the performance.

The rescue crew gathered in Mrs. Cobbler's backyard as the first light of day warmed their pelts. Missy came over and joined Mrs. Cobbler's breakfast ritual. The Choir of Friendly Pets, Chapter 9, serenaded in the front yard. The noise from the choir was just enough to cover the loud tapping noise made by Mr and Mrs Hammer, as they hammered at the rotten window frame. Then Chance and Cleo pushed in the window frame, making an opening wide enough for Binny to access the basement from outside. The animals quietly rejoiced, and Binny made her plan. She couldn't move Moon Girl during the day—someone might see her.

Binny waited patiently all day, making sure no-one would find Moon Girl. She left Moon Girl only long enough to get some food and water. Bedtime couldn't come fast enough. She needed to get Moon Girl into the basement!

Later that night, while everyone was in a deep sleep, Binny moved Moon Girl to the dark, damp basement. Old pieces of furniture were stacked on top of each other, outdated clothes hung on wire racks, piles of boxes towered against the walls, and shelves were filled with unused wrapping paper and forgotten books. No one could find what they were looking for—and probably wouldn't remember the original purpose of entering in the first place. Mrs. Cobbler's basement was certainly not a great option, but it was the most suitable location for Binny to take care of Moon Girl. It would have to do for now.

Chapter 6

AFTER MOVING MOON Girl into the basement, Binny's life became far busier than before.

She had to become invisible when taking food and water to Moon Girl four times a day. And her personal daily grooming time had tripled; every time she cleaned Moon Girl's wrinkly, rough skin, Binny also had to groom herself to get rid of the weird smell. But even as her duties increased, her love for Moon Girl flourished. And she understood that Moon Girl needed more than food and water to survive—she also needed affection. Now, the sole purpose of her life was to nurture Moon Girl.

Moon Girl expressed herself by glowing, giggling, and crying. *Would it be possible to communicate with her with flashing lights by using Morse code?* And so thinking, Binny now had a new goal: Deciphering Moon Girl's language to better understand her needs. At the same time, she would teach her native tongue. *Babies speak by imitating sounds and are capable of learning multiple languages,* she thought, feeling more confident about the future. Hoping her baby's first word would be "mom," she took a mental note to talk to Adel about the translation of flashing light to Morse code.

Besides the language barrier, there were other obstacles. The most significant one was Moon Girl's safety. Each day, Binny considered this and made up new excuses for her disappearance to protect her. She shivered with the thought of someone discovering Moon Girl. Would they report her to the authorities and take her baby girl? *Stop panicking and be smart,* she told herself.

Suddenly, her gut instinct kicked in about Ariel. Over the years, Ariel had become much gentler in her affections. Binny now enjoyed sitting on Ariel's lap for long naps, and Ariel had grown accustomed to Binny accompanying her for walks in the garden.

Yes, Ariel was a darling, but Binny now knew that being a mom was a big responsibility. She would have to make sure Ariel didn't notice that her priorities had changed.

Who could be a good babysitter for Moon Girl while I am entertaining Ariel? Binny thought of asking the Friendly Pets members for help again, but her conscience was wracked by guilt at the thought of leaving Moon Girl to someone else's care. She knew, however, it would not be safe to move Moon Girl to another place in the house.

"Binny, sweetheart," Ariel called out, interrupting her worrying. "Let's go for a walk. Haven't you heard me? I've been calling you all day."

Alarm bells went off in Binny's head. Hastily, she walked to Ariel, realizing her circumstances were getting more dangerous than she imagined.

"Binny, what is going on? You seem tired. Would you rather go inside and read my book with me?" Ariel embraced Binny and walked back toward the house. "I know you like to hear my favorite Nancy Drew mysteries."

Binny despaired and silently followed Ariel, hoping she would soon get bored with her. Finally, in the late afternoon, Binny found an opportunity to slip into the basement with some afternoon snacks for her baby. Moon Girl chuckled and glowed to greet Binny. As soon as Binny put down a cluster of Temptations seafood snacks, Moon Girl rolled on top of the food and munched it quickly.

"Baby, slow down," Binny said, worried about Moon Girl choking.

But Moon Girl just giggled and gave her one long and two short glows that Binny deciphered to mean, "Thank you."

"You're welcome. Mommy loves you so much," Binny crooned, realizing her nightmares hadn't returned since she had saved Moon Girl.

Moon Girl gave her one long, two short, three long, and one brief glow. Binny translated this into, "I love you, too," and her heart filled with love.

Their intuitive powers broke some of the language barriers, but it would still be a long way before she could really understand Moon Girl. *If we spent more time together, understanding each other would improve significantly*, Binny thought. Which was why she didn't want anyone else to watch her baby . . . she just didn't see any other way.

For dinner, Mrs. Cobbler served pork chops with mashed potatoes and green beans. Binny had some dry food, making sure to save some of it for her baby.

By ten o'clock, Mrs. Cobbler had fallen fast asleep on the sofa while watching her favorite show.

"Time for bed. Come on, Binny, follow me," Ariel said.

Binny obeyed. She climbed the stairs, sat at the end of the bed, and watched Ariel fall into a deep sleep. Shortly after, Binny went into the kitchen to get her leftover food and water for Moon Girl. She could only carry one thing at a time in her mouth, so it took multiple trips. She stepped out through her private exit door and headed to the basement where Moon Girl was waiting for her dinner.

Moon Girl greeted her with loud laughs, and Binny had to warn her not to wake up people who were sleeping. She proudly watched as Moon Girl absorbed her dinner in under a minute, and then rolled in the water. Binny realized parenting was the world's most fantastic job.

After finishing her food, Moon Girl sucked in a gust of air, puffed up, glowed brightly, and then bounced over to land two feet ahead of Binny. Then Moon Girl rolled, making distorted meowing mixed with giggling. Binny's eyes widened with happiness and surprise as she watched her baby girl's talents. She predicted Moon Girl soon would pick up her language. For now, it was gibberish, but Binny had high hopes.

Mimicking Moon Girl's jump, Binny sprang toward her, sat down next to the baby, and gently patted her. Moon Girl escaped from her gentle strokes and bounced away, and Binny pounced after her; it seemed they had just invented a mother-daughter bonding game.

"Okay, I'll show you another trick. Watch me." Binny pounced again and gripped her. She rolled her baby with her front paws back and forth, just as she played with Mrs. Cobbler's yarn. Moon Girl giggled for more.

"I'm tired now, but we will play more tomorrow. It is time to rest," Binny crooned, cuddling Moon Girl until they were both fast asleep.

The next morning, Ariel was at the front porch when Binny was attempting to sneak into the house. "Where have you been, Binny? Why are you leaving me alone all the time?"

Binny tried to calm her down with soft meows and gently rubbed her legs.

"You know, Binny, I've been worrying about you a lot," Ariel said. "Being alone outside this early is dangerous."

"You think so?" Binny meowed, thinking Ariel was much more of a threat to her and Moon Girl than her going out alone at dawn.

"Don't you like to be with me anymore, Binny?" Ariel's sorrowful voice was torturing Binny.

"Of course, I love you, dear Ariel," Binny replied, stricken. And while she meant it, her priority was her baby, now.

Binny could see Ariel thought Binny had a big secret and wanted to know what it was. Binny suspected she might even decide to follow Nancy Drew's lead and try to gather evidence. *I'll have to be even more careful,* she thought, feeling sad at the need to withdraw even further from Ariel, but knowing what must be done.

That evening, Binny went outside and asked Polly to send an urgent message to Cleo to meet late in the night. She knew Ariel was watching her behind the curtain in her bedroom window, but Binny had to take the risk.

When Binny returned, Ariel was standing in the hallway. "I'm very sleepy. Come on, Binny. I hope you want to sleep with me tonight."

Binny could hear the sadness of a broken heart in Ariel's voice. She followed her, hoping she quickly went into a deep sleep. And Binny thought she did, after ten minutes of reading. Binny felt secure and went down to give her baby dinner before heading outside.

Chapter 7

AS SOON AS Binny left the room, Ariel got up and tiptoed downstairs. She walked like a cat through the kitchen and watched as Binny put as much food as she could into her cheeks, and grabbed the half full water dish between her teeth, and left the house using her small door flap. Ariel didn't hesitate; she slipped out the door to follow—but Binny moved fast in the darkness with her keen eyes, and Ariel couldn't keep up. She crouched down behind a bush and waited for Binny to reappear in the dark.

The night chill was going into her bones, but Ariel was determined to wait for Binny instead of getting a warm coat from the house. It took longer than she anticipated. Finally, Binny came from the basement window, and Ariel rubbed her eyes, trying to believe what she had just witnessed. Trying to control her breath, she followed Binny.

In the distance, the wind brought low-pitched barking, disrupting the quiet night, and Ariel tried again to calm her breathing. *Thank God—it's only Cleo.* She watched as Binny ran to meet the German shepherd. Ariel took a deep breath, flattened herself against the ground, and crawled closer to listen to their conversation—but all she could hear were tiny snippets, one of which was "Moon Girl." *Moon Girl? Who is Moon Girl?* she wondered.

At one point, Ariel panicked, seeing Binny peering through the darkness toward her, but she breathed a sigh of relief when Binny merely turned back to Cleo. Exhausted, realizing she wasn't learning anything new at this point, she crawled back to the house, cleaned herself, and went back to bed. It was hard to sleep. Thoughts whirled in her head as she tried to make sense of what she had seen; it was a wild mystery without any reasonable explanation. She rolled to her side, covered her head with the blanket, and tried to fall asleep.

Before long, Binny crept in, jumped up to Ariel's bed, and laid on top of her. Ariel rolled over and whispered, "Good night, Binny."

It was hard to sleep while so many questions were swirling in her head. *What I saw tonight . . . has it happened before?* As she tried to organize her thoughts, her head ached with the effort. Feeling feverish, Ariel gently eased herself out from under Binny, got up, and went into the bathroom to splash her face with cold water. When she returned to the bed, Binny's emerald eyes were staring at her. *This isn't a dream. This is real.*

Ariel got up late, awakened by bright sunlight shimmering in and reflecting from her dresser mirror. Binny was long gone. She took a quick shower, brushed her hair, put on her overalls, and went to the kitchen for Auntie's delicious blueberry pancake breakfast, planning to go down to the basement next.

"GOOD MORNING," BINNY greeted Ariel as the girl devoured her blueberry pancakes.

Last night's meeting with Cleo eased her worries, and she was feeling cheery. When she had explained her quandary to Cleo and asked if there was anyone she knew that might be willing to keep Moon Girl safe and happy while Binny spent time with Ariel, Cleo had given it some serious consideration, and Binny had tried not to fidget as the large dog pondered. Cleo eventually suggested that Missy take care of Moon Girl while Binny was with Ariel; Cleo and the rest of the club members would watch for suspicious activity near the basement window.

"Hello, there, my partner in crime," Ariel crooned as she bent down to pet Binny. Mrs. Cobbler's eyes lit with interest, but Ariel merely gazed into Binny's eyes. She picked her up, and with a big grin, asked, "Aren't you, Binny?"

Binny's stomach leaped into her throat, and she wondered if Ariel had secretly followed her last night, thinking of some rustling she'd heard in the bushes. *But . . . but she was in a deep sleep . . . wasn't she?* she thought, frantically. She leaned forward to nuzzle Ariel's chest without looking at her face. She felt guilty for betraying her, but she didn't know how else to protect her baby.

Chapter 8

"YOU HAVEN'T FINISHED your breakfast, Ariel," Mrs. Cobbler said as Ariel stood up.

"Thank you, Auntie. I'm stuffed," she said, thinking that the only way to find out Binny's secret was to inspect the basement to see what Binny was hiding from her. Tilting her head, she asked, "Auntie, I'd like to donate some of my old books to charity. Are they in the basement?"

"Oh, what a great idea. I haven't been down there for a long time, though. You are welcome to take what you need. I can help you, if you'd like," Mrs. Cobbler added.

"Please, Auntie, don't bother going down. It would hurt your joints too much. But can I borrow your flashlight?"

Mrs. Cobbler rubbed her knees. "Well, dear, I suppose you are right. My knees do hurt quite a bit these days. The flashlight is in the laundry room closet, next to the washing machine. Check the batteries first."

Ariel kissed Mrs. Cobbler's cheek and tried to contain her excitement, telling herself this wasn't a murder mystery, like one of Nancy Drew's, to be solved. She walked to the laundry room, found the flashlight, checked the batteries, and walked down the stairs to the basement.

She was flabbergasted by all the stacks of furniture, racks of dusty clothes, and overflowing shelves filled with books and old pots. There was no doubt that Auntie Cobbler was a junk keeper, a hoarder.

Looking at the mountains of useless items, she felt overwhelmed. How could she find a shred of evidence in this mess? The damp, moldy air filled her lungs, and her throat itched. Feeling hopeless,

Ariel walked back to the stairs, bumping into something on her way.

She heard a giggle and spun around, then saw a glittering light on the wall. Eyes wide, she mumbled, "Hello?" Then, pointing her flashlight toward the glint, she moved closer to it—and gasped.

It was a glowing ball. Ariel froze as fear reverberated through her body, her heart pounding violently. Panic gripped her as the thing continued giggling and flashing. The thing's skin kind of sparkled, its arms on the top moved towards to grab her. Ariel wanted to do something, say something, but she was speechless in her terror. She took a deep breath, shifted her weight from one foot to another, and slowly walked backward until she reached the stairs. Giving the thing one last glance, Ariel turned and fled, thinking, *Binny has a lot of explaining to do.*

She felt utterly alone and betrayed. *Was this Binny's secret?* she wondered, hoping there was some reasonable explanation behind all this. By lunchtime, she was calm and had organized her thoughts, ready to question Binny.

ARIEL WAS SETTING the table for lunch when Binny showed up in the kitchen She padded over to Ariel and rubbed against her legs.

Ariel quickly stepped back, frowning. "What are you hiding in the basement, Binny?"

Binny glanced around to make sure Mrs. Cobbler wasn't in earshot. "I . . . um. Don't know what are you talking about?" She looked away.

Ariel took a deep breath. "Don't be silly. Do you think you can hide things from me? Besides—I followed you last night. So, tell me—what is that strange thing you've got in the basement?"

Binny paced for a moment, then stopped and narrowed her eyes as she looked at Ariel. "I don't think it's good for you to know. I don't want to put you in danger, Ariel."

Ariel's eyes widened slightly. "Danger?" But before Binny could explain, Mrs. Cobbler walked into the kitchen. Ariel leaned down and whispered, "Don't disappear. We have to talk."

On the verge of an emotional breakdown, Binny meowed, "Um . . . I'll be right back!" and before Ariel could argue, she rushed off to see Cleo for some desperately needed advice.

Binny found Cleo sitting in front of Dr. Andreas's office, enjoying the sunny April afternoon.

"I got caught by Ariel, Cleo," Binny said, without even saying hello.

Cleo stood up and shook, jingling her collar. "Is Moon Girl still safe?"

"I don't know. I didn't tell Ariel the whole story, yet. But she won't give up until she gets what she wants."

"Just tell her the truth, then. The only way to keep Moon Girl safe is to convince Ariel that your baby is harmless. You are brave. Don't lose your faith. Go. Tell her the whole story."

Hearing Cleo's advice was a relief. Binny regained her confidence, thanked her, and took a shortcut home to talk to Ariel.

Chapter 9

BINNY WALKED INTO the room and sat in front of Ariel.

Ariel put her book down on the coffee table. "I'm ready to hear your story, now."

"Moon Girl came from the sky," Binny began after a moment, "and she won't hurt anyone. I love my baby very much. Please keep my secret safe."

Ariel could hear the relief in Binny's voice at revealing her secret . . . although it was a shocking story for Ariel to swallow.

Is Binny delirious? "How can you expect me to believe this, Binny?" she asked. "Bring me to her, please."

Binny swallowed hard. "Alright then. We can go down after dinner when Auntie tunes in to her favorite TV shows."

For the rest of the day, both Binny and Ariel impatiently waited for Mrs. Cobbler's eyes to finally be glued to the TV.

After dinner, Ariel excused herself, saying she was going to bed early, and gave her aunt a goodnight kiss and hug. Then she grabbed the flashlight and whispered to Binny, "It's time. I opened the basement door for you. You go down first. I'll close the basement door behind us."

Ariel listened as Binny crept to the kitchen, got Moon Girl's dinner and water, and then she followed as Binny slunk down the stairs to the basement.

The glowing ball giggled at Binny's arrival, bouncing toward her. Standing just behind Binny, Ariel was breathless yet remained silent as she watched Binny drop her leftover dinner to the floor. The thing bounced up and landed on top of the food pile, crunching it up in a minute, glowing while she ate.

Ariel stumbled backward. "Is this a dream?" she whispered, pinching her own arm.

Binny glanced at Ariel. "Yes, this is real. This is Moon Girl, and she won't hurt you. Don't be scared of her."

Ariel stared at her, bewildered. "This is . . . incredible."

"My sweet girl won't endanger anyone. She glows peacefully and is happy here. Can I keep her, please, Ariel?"

Ariel took a deep breath. "Is it safe to hold her?"

"Yes, certainly. Let me introduce you. Moon Girl would love to meet you."

Binny sat next to Moon Girl, gazed down calmly, and touched the glowing creature gently with one paw. "Hey, sweetie. This is Ariel, my best human friend. Is it okay if she holds you?"

Moon Girl bounced softly under her paw with a whooshing sound. Ariel picked up Moon Girl and held her gingerly. Moon Girl released a soft, flashing light, giggling happily.

Ariel gently touched Moon Girl. "Her skin is moist and shiny yet looks old and wrinkly. Are you sure it is a baby, Binny?"

"HER OUTSIDE MAY be old and creased, Ariel. But inside, there is a lovely young soul happy to be with me."

Ariel placed Moon Girl on the floor and fixed her eyes on the Moon Girl's frayed, tangled arms, "Hmm! It is very odd, Binny. Moon Girl's arms look like a bunch of threads bound together. Reminds me of something I'm very familiar with. But I can't think what it is."

Binny pinned back her ears and padded toward Moon Girl, "I think her arms were injured when she fell off from the sky, Ariel. She can only move her arms when she leaps. We have something in common, don't you think? An accident . . ."

Ariel kneed down and touched the shiny grains. "Red sand with a musty smell."

She shrugged her shoulder. "Weird discharge. Could Moon Girl be an alien who came from Mars?"

Binny crouched down next to Ariel and licked her finger, feeling salt taste in her back of the throat. "She has a unique discharge making her lose her round shape no matter how much she eats or drinks. That makes me worry about her health. It doesn't matter if my girl is an alien. I love her, and she loves me too."

Having not received a response , Binny tried again. "Can Moon Girl live with me, Ariel? Would you please keep my secret safe?"

Happy with her first attempt at detective work—but knowing she had a long way to go before she mastered her skills—Ariel looked into Binny's eyes and smiled. "You don't need to worry anymore, Binny. Your secret is safe with me."

Chapter 10

EVER SINCE ARIEL had promised to keep her secret safe, Binny felt much better, assuming that the worst was over. Binny's heart felt lighter, and she had thanked Ariel, but she still couldn't help but worry about what other struggles could be ahead, and whether or not she could protect her baby's life.

In a flash, Ariel became Moon Girl's play partner. But she kept her doubts about Moon Girl's discharge that deformed her body day by day. She wondered about the tangled arms she had seen before, similar to the knotted cords. She wrote down a list of descriptions to investigate at the town's library.

Binny enjoyed watching their nightly hide-and-seek game in the backyard after Mrs. Cobbler retired to her bedroom. In this game, sometimes Binny was the seeker, but most of the time, she was home base. Moon Girl quickly learned to control her glowing and dim herself, which made it challenging to find her. Ariel would search tirelessly under shrubs and behind dwarf pine trees until Moon Girl flashed her light, as if saying, "I'm here! Come catch me if you can." She would then dim her light, suck in air, and blow it out to bounce around the background of shadows, from bushes to trees, until the count of thirty was over. Then, with her flashing glow, she would spring to home base, making Binny laugh.

Toward the middle of the week, Binny had a sudden urge to talk to Polly, the friendly cardinal, who was singing to her eggs, waiting for them to hatch.

"Have you ever felt so happy and lucky about your life," Binny asked Polly, "but also scared that something will happen to ruin it and turn everything upside down?"

"Nonsense," Polly said with a ruffle of her feathers. "You deserve happiness like everyone else. I have an idea." She adjusted one of her eggs. "Instead of thinking like a drama queen, why don't you throw a party to introduce your baby, as I've done each year? It'll be good for your soul, dear."

Binny smiled. "You are right. I forgot all about our club's rules to introduce new offspring to our members—thanks for reminding me. I can see you have your feathers full, so I'll fetch Cleo to help arrange a celebration party. Good luck, Polly."

One of the best advantages of having a good friend who lived with a vet was that they had access to all area pets. Cleo happily propagated the news about Binny's celebration party for Moon Girl, to take place the following night at nine o'clock.

"Would it be okay to cancel tomorrow night's game, Ariel? I will be presenting Moon Girl to our club members," Binny asked.

"Well, it's about time. I wondered when this would finally happen," Ariel said, and then laughed. "It'll be like having a baby shower—but after the baby arrives. And of course, I don't mind. But promise me you'll tell me every detail about the party—and make sure Cleo escorts you two through the woods."

Binny readily agreed to the terms with a smile.

The next night, Ariel gave Binny her old Easter basket to carry Moon Girl safely to the celebration party. They both went to the basement to place Moon Girl into the basket, and then Binny whisked her tail, grasped the basket in her mouth, and climbed out the window to meet Cleo, who had been digging at the dried grass to announce her presence.

She greeted Binny and murmured, "You look stunning. Your happiness suits you." Seemingly excited about escorting her and Moon Girl, Cleo kept her eyes on the path, tracking bushes and trees to spot any possible threat.

Binny thought this would be a small, informal gathering. So, she was surprised to see the large crowd on the west side of the park by Horton Lake. Almost all the members were there, eager to see her baby who had come from the sky.

Chance cleared his throat with a quick bark. "Ladies and Gentlemen, order, please. Let's form a circle—Miss Binny and her baby Moon Girl have just arrived."

Binny slowly and proudly walked into the middle of the circle and placed her basket on the ground amidst applause. Binny gazed at all the happy faces and swished her tail proudly. "Ladies and Gentlemen, meet my baby, Moon Girl."

Everyone stood up and sang a greeting song for Moon Girl:

We wish you a long life, Moon Girl.
You have our love and prayers,
and a happy and healthy beating heart.
Welcome to us from the sky.

Binny took her baby out from the basket, held her gently in her mouth, and bowed to the audience. "Thank you for your beautiful song, my friends. My baby is thrilled to meet you."

Moon Girl flashed sparkling lights on all of their furry faces. As her lights scattered over the group, many of the pets shivered in fear, and murmurs of alarm rolled through the group.

"Order, please," Chance called out. "Let's continue our celebration. Please take turns showering the baby with your gifts." Then he placed a bell into the basket. "Nudge this bell to call your mom when you need her—she'll be visiting with her friends here."

The party was perfect. And at the end of the celebration, Chance presented a birth certificate for Moon Girl. "Cleo got this from Dr. Andreas's office. I'm sure Ariel will help you fill it out."

Binny could hardly control her tears. "Thank you, all," she said, looking down into Moon Girl's basket—which was so full of gifts that Binny had a hard time carrying it.

"I can carry your basket, Binny," Cleo offered.

"What would I do without you?" Binny exclaimed.

"No worries, dear," Cleo said, taking the handle of the basket in her jaws.

Binny took a deep breath. "Lead the way home, my friend."

They both padded away, their paws barely making a sound in the night air.

Chapter 11

THE NEXT DAY, Binny rushed into the kitchen and leaped onto Ariel's lap. Her bright green eyes brimming with tears, she placed her front paws on the girl's chest.

"Oh, Ariel—please come quick. My baby—oh, she is in such pain. Please help her, Ariel."

Ariel gasped and sprang from the chair. They headed straight down to the basement, where they found Moon Girl lying flat on the floor.

Terrified, Binny reached down to embrace her and nudged her gently with her mouth. "She's gotten even worse," she meowed in dismay.

Moon Girl moaned, hearing Binny's voice.

Ariel was also frightened. With tears in her eyes, she took a deep breath and asked, "Who can help us? Think, Binny."

Binny was silent for a moment, trying to think through her panic. "I . . . I just don't know. Cleo, maybe? Her owner is a vet . . ."

Ariel thought hard. "I'll stay down here with Moon Girl and do an Internet search on my phone, and you go to Cleo."

Binny raced to Cleo's house.

"Moon Girl is very sick," she meowed, once Cleo came outside. "Can you please help my baby?"

Cleo frowned. "What is wrong with her, love?"

"She's shaking, and she's just lying flat out on the floor," Binny cried. "She doesn't shine or glow—and it all happened so suddenly. I don't know what to do and where to go. You are wiser than everyone else, Cleo—you've seen sick pets at Dr. Andreas's clinic. Please, please, help us."

Cleo licked Binny's face. "Try to breathe, Binny. Panicking won't help. I'll do what I can, but . . . Moon Girl is a unique case.

We can sneak into Dr. Andreas's office tonight to search his books and find out if there is a cure for her illness."

Binny choked back a sob. "Tonight? I'm afraid that will be too late. Can we go in now?"

Cleo raised one of her front paws to Binny's face and wiped her spilled tears. "Ok, Binny. He just went on his lunch break, but we must be quick. We'll have less than an hour."

She guided Binny to the back of the house shaded with maple trees bordering the yard. Cleo pushed the half-opened window with her front paws and then helped Binny in. The office was small, but the layout was neat—Cleo pointed to a bookshelf. "That's it. I hope we find what we are looking for." She jumped to an office chair and peered at the top shelf. After reading the book titles—*Merck Veterinary Manual, Veterinary Drug Handbook, Veterinary Anatomy*—she pulled two thick books from the shelf, one at a time, with her teeth. "I'll start with *Merck's Manual*. You check *Veterinary Anatomy* for any descriptions that match Moon Girl."

She glanced at Binny. "I wish I could have read *Merck's* before. It has plenty of useful information about the animal kingdom and cures for diseases."

The two nosed through the pages as quickly as possible.

"Anything useful?" Cleo whispered after a while.

"Nothing," Binny replied without looking up.

"We don't have much time. Keep searching, and hurry."

"How can I scan thousands of pages in less than an hour? It's not possible," Binny moaned.

"I wish there was some way to get the books out of the office," Cleo lamented as she continued her frantic search through the pages. Just then, Dr. Andreas stepped into the room.

"Well, now. Can I help you, folks?" he said, walking toward Cleo with a chuckle, glancing around at the two books scattered on the floor through the thick lenses of his glasses. "What you two up to?" He put his hands in his white coat pockets, still smiling. Then he picked up his books and placed them back on the bookshelf.

"Interested in veterinary medicine, are we?" He looked from Cleo to Binny.

Cleo turned to Binny, her eyes apologetic. "Let's try again tonight."

"Ok—I have to go now," Binny whispered and then jumped up on the desk and out the open window.

Chapter 12

BINNY GOT HOME and found Ariel sitting at the top of the basement stairs.

"Any good news?" Binny asked, eagerly.

Ariel's shoulders slumped. "When I searched for 'glowing ball,' all I got were advertisements for things like LED garden ball sets, and then the 'glowing ball of light' search only came up with stuff like *Russian scientists spotted glowing orbs of light throughout Siberia.*" She sighed and then looked thoughtful. "I wonder if Moon Girl was part of a Russian covert operation . . . I should start my investigation sooner when I noticed her losing her shape and dimming her light. She might be an alien from Mars. Have you found any clues?"

Binny whimpered. "No luck. Dr. Andreas caught us. We'll try again tonight."

Ariel picked Binny up and gently smoothed her spiky fur. "I'll go to the library today to search more—and then I want to come with you tonight, Binny."

Binny pointed her ears, shaking her head. "No. It is too dangerous. I don't want you to get into trouble, Ariel."

"I have decided already. I want to help save Moon Girl. Your baby is my friend," Ariel said firmly.

"Sweetie, the chocolate chip cookies are ready. Come on up and have some," Mrs. Cobbler called down from the kitchen.

Ariel sighed. "I have to go. I think Auntie suspects something is going on, Binny. She's been saying things like 'What's happened to my chatty girl,' and 'You and Binny have been awfully secretive lately.'" She turned and headed up the stairs. "You stay with Moon Girl. After dinner, I'll call to you through the window and we can meet at the front porch."

Ariel went up to the kitchen, and Binny crossed the room to Moon Girl.

"How are you, baby?" Binny softly meowed.

Moon Girl attempted to get up from the floor, but she collapsed, unable to hold herself up.

Binny's voice cracked as she tried to soothe her baby. "Hang on, love—we'll find your cure. This will be over soon." She picked a bag of soft Whisker Licking snacks from the shower gift basket and offered some to Moon Girl. "Try to eat a bit, to gain your strength."

Moon Girl could only moan, and her response shattered Binny's heart. She cuddled her baby in her paws and sang a lullaby, trying to ease her pain. Moon Girl snuggled into her.

Binny scratched herself and bit her nails. She was in a prickle of uneasiness, wondering why time was moving at a snail's pace, and she desperately stared at the window, waiting for Ariel.

Chapter 13

THE NAUVOO PUBLIC Library was a two-story building next to the town's laundromat. Ariel's ten-minute walk to the library seemed longer, as the town had been seized by a heatwave. Nevertheless, the streets were busy with airy excitement preparing for next week's music festival.

Feeling secure, seeing familiar faces, Ariel smiled and greeted Auntie's neighbors on the road on her way to the library. Ariel was about to faint when she finally arrived at the library's narrow entrance, and she swiped her forehead before stepping into the small hall.

"Ariel, what a nice surprise. Happy to see you, sweetie," Miss Teresa, the librarian, greeted.

"Good afternoon, Miss Teresa. I'm looking for information about a glowing ball?"

Miss Teresa raised an eyebrow. "You mean like an ornament, or a beach ball, dear?"

Ariel shook her head. "No. Actually, I'm looking for how to cure a sick glowing ball."

"Hmm," Miss Teresa murmured, brows furrowed. "Do you mean how to *repair* a glowing ball, dear?"

Ariel shut her eyes for a moment. "I—I don't know . . . what it is."

Miss Teresa chuckled. "No worries, dear. Either way, you are at the right place. We have all kinds of repair manuals to help you." She bustled off, returned a few moments later, and handed Ariel a small leaflet. "Here you go, dear."

Ariel's hopes soared until she realized what she had in her hands were instructions for repairing and changing LED lights. At a loss of what more she could research, she decided to research

Dr. Andreas to see if he was trained to look after rare species of animals. But all she could see was where he went to university, and information about his clinic. Feeling hopeless, she walked back home, empty-handed.

AFTER WHAT SEEMED like hours and hours, Ariel finally called to Binny. Binny padded over to Moon Girl, leaned over, and whispered, "Hang on, my brave girl. I'll save you." Then she twitched her tail and arched her back to leap to the basement window to meet Ariel.

"Did you find anything helpful at the library?" Binny meowed.

Ariel gave her a dejected shrug. "Nothing useful," she said with a sigh. "Just some stuff about the doctor."

"Like what?"

"Well, like I said," Ariel replied. "Nothing earth-shattering. He graduated from the College of Veterinary Medicine at Urbana-Champaign and then worked at Fort Madison, Iowa, for ten years. Then he bought the building he's in now and established The Friendly Pets Clinic. He planned the whole renovation himself to change the house into the clinic. The first floor is the clinic, and the second floor is his home."

On their way to to meet Cleo, they ran under the curtain of trees, striving to be invisible, and took shortcuts with a sense of added urgency. They crossed Main Street and headed around to the back of the clinic.

"Why is she here?" Cleo growled, looking at Ariel.

"Ariel insisted on coming," Binny meowed.

Ariel gave a quick wink. "No time to discuss. How do we get in the office?"

"The back window is always open. Just follow me," Cleo said, and guided them over to the window. "Step up here and slide in."

Once inside, Binny's keen eyes spotted the bookshelf in the dark. "Can you get us the *Merck Manual* and the anatomy books, Ariel?"

Ariel turned on her flashlight and stepped on the chair to reach the top shelf, but the books slipped out of her hands and fell to the floor with a crash.

"Hide under the table," Cleo ordered.

They waited in the dark for approaching footsteps. All was silent, though, except for the sounds of their heavy panting. Cleo stood, her ears erect. "We got lucky."

Cleo grasped the *Merck Manual* and started reading, and Binny got into anatomy pages with Ariel.

"My eyes are getting blurry," Cleo whined. "Ariel, can you point your flashlight toward my pages a bit?"

"Ariel, sit between us. I can use your light, too," Binny suggested.

After an eternity of speed-reading, Ariel sighed. "Aren't there any chapters in these books about rare species?"

Binny flipped to the table of contents. "None."

"Same here," Cleo confirmed.

"We are wasting time," Ariel said with another deep sigh.

The room suddenly lit up, and a man in pajamas stood there, his white hair standing in spikes on his head.

"Don't move! Hands up!" he shouted.

Binny felt her heart stop when she realized it was Doctor Andreas pointing a gun.

"Don't shoot," Ariel whimpered.

"Ariel, is that you?" His jaws dropped as he took in the sight of the trio. "What are you doing here, for God's sake?" He lowered the gun, pursed his lips, and walked toward Cleo and Binny. "You two, again? This is the second time I've found you in my office today, shuffling through my books. Now, it seems you've recruited this little lady." He approached Ariel and clasped her hands. "Ariel, what you are looking for? I don't think your aunt would be pleased, hearing you're out in the middle of the night and breaking into my office."

Binny's ears were erect and her fur became spiky. "Don't say anything."

Cleo whined. "Maybe he can help, Binny."

Ariel's face burning with shame, and she mouthed *I'm sorry* to Binny before turning back to the doctor. "My apologies for tonight, Dr. Andreas . . . but our intentions were good. Binny's baby is very sick, you see. Please, help us."

Doctor Andreas's eyebrows went up. "What are you talking about, Ariel? Binny doesn't have any kittens. She isn't able to."

"She adopted a thing that came from the sky. Please, don't tell my aunt," Ariel added, pleading.

Doctor Andreas gave Ariel a look, and then finally pointed to the door. "Go home and get some sleep; come by first thing in the morning, and we'll sort out this nonsense."

Ariel and Binny quickly left the office.

Ariel picked up Binny and started walking fast—as if she walked quickly enough and got far enough away from the clinic, tonight's incident would not have happened at all. The night was dark, still, and quiet. After walking a couple of blocks, Ariel stopped to breathe and asked, "Are we good, Binny? Because you must realize that Doctor Andreas is our only chance. Please don't blame me for asking him to help."

"Oh, I know, Ariel—and it was courageous of you to speak up, especially after I told you not to. But I'm losing hope. I will do anything to see my girl healthy again," Binny cried.

Ariel lowered her head and touched her lips to Binny's wet cheeks. "Don't cry, please. You are an excellent mother."

Binny gazed into Ariel's eyes with a mournful smile. "I'm lucky to have a friend like you."

Wrapping her arms around Binny, Ariel buried her face in her spiky pelt. "Tomorrow will be a good day for us. Let's try and get some sleep."

When they arrived back at the house, Ariel gave her a hug and whispered, "Our Moon Girl will be fine. Don't worry, Binny."

Chapter 14

BINNY TOSSED IN her sleep, worried about what Dr. Andreas would say when he saw Moon Girl. He was an outsider—not like her best friend, Ariel. She twisted her body away from Ariel, trying not to wake her with her constant rolling. At dawn, Binny finally fell into a half-sleep.

In her dreams, she flew over thick clouds. With a sudden drop, she landed in a musty, dark room where Moon Girl was being held captive in a glass bowl, sobbing and wailing for help. Binny sprinted toward the glass bowl and leaped into the air to rescue her baby. But as she tried to reach out, the bowl imprisoning Moon Girl moved farther away. Binny cried her name, again and again. Her baby's wails filled her head as the glass bowl faded up and vanished into the smoke clouds, and Binny howled herself awake from the horrible nightmare. It was morning, and a cold shiver seized her exhausted body; it took ten tail lengths to control her breathing. Her whiskers twitched in panic.

Ariel was awakened by Binny's howl. "What happened?" she asked, rubbing her eyes.

"I . . . I had a nightmare," Binny murmured.

They both scurried down to the basement to check Moon Girl. Binny nudged Moon Girl's deflated form. Her baby whimpered. "No change," Binny meowed.

"At least she is not getting worse," Ariel said. She placed Moon Girl in a basket and covered her. "Let's pray this will be over soon. Come on—we need to be there on time, Binny."

They struck out, hoping to be home before Mrs. Cobbler got up. Binny sauntered along with her usual crooked gait, leaning to her strong side and wincing as she struggled to speed up.

"I can carry you, Binny," Ariel said. "I'm strong enough to hold both of you."

"No worries, Ariel. I can manage," Binny replied.

When they arrived at the doctor's office, Binny's legs were shaking. Ariel bit her lip and wrung her hands, but Binny could see she was trying to be brave.

"At least we're not breaking in this time. Our visit is legit," she said with a nervous smile.

Once they were in the examination room with Dr. Andreas, Ariel laid the basket on the exam table.

"Can you cure her?" Ariel asked, sounding hopeful as he uncovered the basket and looked inside.

After a few moments, his eyes flared with anger. "Is this a joke? I am a busy man—I have patients that need my help."

"No, Dr. Andreas—this is Moon Girl, Binny's baby girl. We swear. She was jumping, glowing, and giggling, just two days ago. Now she just lies there," Ariel said, near tears.

Binny wailed and nodded. "She is telling the truth, Doctor."

Dr. Andreas peered into Ariel's face. Finally, he nodded and winked, taking Moon Girl from the basket and placing her on the examination table. Binny could see he was just playing along, but she figured it was a start. "First," he began, taking out a thermometer and prodding at Moon Girl with its tip, "we need to check her temperature." He waited until it beeped and then smiled crookedly. "Hey, look, she doesn't have a fever." He pursed his lips and shot them both a look. "Should I cut into her and look inside?"

Binny yowled, and Ariel shrieked, grabbing his arm in alarm.

"How do you want me to save her, Ariel, without looking inside your friend?" he said. "How am I supposed to diagnose her?"

"I don't know, sir. But I know she is alive. Please—please don't hurt her." Ariel softly touched Moon Girl, and whispered, "Show us you are alive, dear one. Glow for us, please." Her tears dripped onto Moon Girl's skin. But minutes passed, and Ariel dropped her arm. Avoiding eye contact, she turned away, murmuring through her tears, "I'm so sorry, Doctor Andreas, but . . . we have no proof. I'm . . ."

A dim light, accompanied by a burbling groan, interrupted her. She whirled around and staring at Moon Girl, and a tearful smile spread across her face.

Binny gave a quavering *meow* of relief.

"You've got your proof, Doc," Ariel said, wiping her tears. "So, what happens next?"

Dr. Andreas was wide-eyed and breathless but quickly regained his composure. "You'd better not be recording all this right now, because if anyone ever saw this, I'd be locked away." He donned his latex gloves, adjusted his glasses, and inspected Moon Girl's skin.

"It looks like faded, tanned hide," he said.

"What does that mean?" Ariel asked.

"Processed animal skin. Because of the faded color, I believe its skin was treated with oak bark and then sun-dried. What I don't understand is why it feels slippery and smells like the ocean or a salt marsh."

"It is odd—I mean, Moon Girl fell from the sky," Ariel said.

"Yes, it is bizarre." Dr. Andreas gave another sniff. "It almost smells like DMS."

Ariel raised an eyebrow.

"Dimethyl sulfide," he explained. "I took a course on marine mammals in college. You see, there are microscopic organisms in water called phytoplankton. They are tiny and hard to spot with the naked eye, Ariel. They use the sun's light to remove carbon dioxide from the water, benefiting other aquatic species during the process. When plankton dies, the bacteria living inside of it produces DMS. That's the refreshing smell of the ocean. Plankton use dimethylsulfoniopropionate, or DMSP, as a sort of sunscreen to protect themselves. Perhaps its skin was soaked in the sea or a salt marsh for a very long time."

Ariel looked at Binny and shrugged. Binny didn't understand his scientific talk either. They watched him, eyes wide in panic.

The doctor inspected Moon Girl's tassel-shaped arms and then stopped to take a picture with his camera. "In case I need to re-tie them," he explained, giving them a half-smile. "Now, I'll find out if you guys are playing me." He untangled the strands one by one.

Binny tensed her muscles for a leap and landed on the exam table, meowing ferociously.

Dr. Andreas jumped. "Whoa! What are you doing, Binny?"

Ariel reached out to calm Binny. "Let the doctor examine her. Please, Binny, trust me. He won't do any harm."

Cleo entered the room, padded over to Binny, and nuzzled her face. "It's true. Be calm, Binny. I think Doc might come up with the cure."

Dr. Andreas paused and smiled at Binny. "Relax. I'm just untangling the knots. They can be re-tied if you wish."

He separated the tangles one by one. "The arms are the same material—tanned hide."

He used a solution to smooth them and then powdered each one to prevent re-tangling. He used forceps to gently work at the tangled strands, tracing each one painstakingly back to its origin before easing it free, loosening and tugging until the knot's heart came apart and opened, revealing a mysterious pile of reddish grains.

"What's this?" he murmured, eyes widening. Taking a deep breath, he inspected the mound.

Binny, Cleo, and Ariel stared, flabbergasted. Ariel struggled for words. "I . . . I'm pretty sure—no, I know there was something inside, glowing and giggling."

Binny mewled piteously beside her in agreement.

Dr. Andreas gently dug into the pile and inspected it, using his magnifier.

"Is she . . . gone?" Binny asked Ariel, barely able to speak.

Ariel gently wrapped Binny into her arms. "Hold tight. Doctor Andreas will find your baby."

Their eyes glued on the doctor's tedious work, they waited impatiently for a miracle.

Chapter 15

AFTER WHAT SEEMED like hours, Dr. Andreas plucked a small, curled up thing out of the ball of red sand and frizz with his forceps. "Voila! It was wrapped up inside the ball with the red sand."

Ariel raised an eyebrow. "Um . . . what is it?"

"It looks like some kind of fish or sea animal," he said with a shrug.

"Is it . . . alive?" Ariel asked.

Dr. Andreas walked to the faucet next to the cabinet, filled a glass bowl with water and added some of the reddish grains from the pile on the table where he had been working. "It is a fish from the sea, so it needs these red grains of sea salt. It isn't really enough, but it should help to keep it alive for a little while."

He held the curled up fish with his forceps, and gently put it into the bowl, and watched for a moment until it moved. "It is alive. It will need more sea salt later to survive."

Binny flinched in shock. "Is my baby girl . . . a fish? How can a fish fall from the sky?" she murmured in awe to her friends.

Cleo shrugged. "I have no idea. But I trust the doc."

Ariel gazed into the glass bowl in shock. She squinted at the little thing, swimming in slow motion. "But... Binny gave her water all the time. Why did she get sick?"

Dr. Andreas continued, "The tap water didn't have sea salt in it. So it was the wrong kind of water. Drinking water needs a large amount of sea salt and minerals to make up the right kind of water for it to survive. Also, the water temperature has to be right in order to dissolve the salt and minerals that we add to it. If the water is too cold, the salt won't melt in the water."

Ariel eyes widened, "Wow! What kind of fish is she, Doc?"

"I'm not an expert in marine animals, but I will do some research if you leave it here for me to study for a couple of days. I'm not sure if your fish will survive that long, because we don't have any sea water near us that we can use."

Binny fluffed up her fur, raised her short, crooked tail, and gave a low yowl from deep in her throat.

Swallowing hard, Ariel tore her eyes from Binny and nodded. "Okay, Dr. Andreas."

Binny yowled again.

"I'll let you know about my findings soon. Now, if you excuse me, little lady, I have patients that require my care."

Binny's ears twitched, and she felt dizzy. Devastated, she padded over to the bowl to nuzzle at the glass. "So long, my baby girl. Stay well," she mewed, and Moon Girl swam close to the glass, touching her face to where Binny's nose rested on the glass. Then, despondent, Binny followed Ariel and Cleo, not even realizing her legs were moving.

Once they left the building, Ariel looked down at her. "I'm so sorry, Binny. I couldn't wait for your reply. We had to act fast to save her."

Binny looked down, hiding her eyes from Ariel, trying to disguise the tidal wave of despair and sadness that overtook her. "I just . . ." she mewed in a tiny voice. "I just can't stop my instincts that he is not looking out for Moon Girl's best interests." Everything seemed unreal, and she sank deeper into misery. "I know you trust him—but I just can't. I feel so alone." A tear trickled down her furry face.

Ariel embraced her, her eyes filled with love. "You aren't alone. We'll do whatever it takes to save Moon Girl."

Binny pulled away. "I know you are my friend, and that you've always been ready to help. But it feels like the rest of the world doesn't think I deserve such happiness."

In Binny's past, all those years of trying to have a family, made her feel like she was a failure. And now, despite this chance she'd been given, it felt like she'd failed again. Her hopes and dreams faded as she followed Ariel across Main Street.

"But thank you," she murmured, trying to muster up some optimism. "I hope my instincts are wrong about the doctor."

"So do I," Ariel whispered, kissing Binny on her forehead. She stood up and gave a little chuckle. "Surreal, huh? That whole thing was freaky. Trust me, my friend. The doctor will save your girl. You will be with her soon."

Binny's legs ached from taking so many long excursions around town; extended periods of walking were never her strength. Limping in pain, she replayed all of her memories of Moon Girl, from the night she brought her home, right up to this morning— when she had learned her precious baby was actually a fish. She glanced up at some kids playing hopscotch on the sidewalk. "Why me? Why my baby?"

They headed toward the house in silence, feeling each other's pain, until Mrs. Cobbler flung open the front door.

"Where did you go, Ariel? You've been gone for hours—I had no idea where you were. I'm afraid I'll have to call your parents." Her big blue eyes were creased with worry.

Ariel gasped, and Binny knew it would be her worst nightmare to have her dad take her home before the end of spring break; it would be a total lockdown for the rest of her vacation.

"I'm so sorry for scaring you, dear Auntie. Binny was not feeling well. I took her to see Dr. Andreas."

Her story is mostly true, Binny thought guiltily.

Mrs. Cobbler took Binny in her arms. "Oh. Again? What did Dr. Andreas say? Ariel, you should have told me. I could have driven you." She gave Binny a warm hug.

"It was nothing," Ariel said. "The doctor said Binny was just a bit under the weather. I'm really sorry, Auntie, but I didn't want you to have to get up early."

"Well, thank you—but next time, you should tell me where you are going, or leave me a note. I don't want you wandering around town alone."

"Yes, Auntie."

"Alright then . . . now, you must be starving, dear. There's French toast on the table."

Ariel's stomach gurgled with hunger, and she rushed to the kitchen. Binny released herself from Mrs. Cobbler's arms to follow Ariel, even though she had no appetite.

That night Ariel embraced Binny and went to sleep quickly. Her smell of lavender soap and her warm arms could not ease Binny's anxiety. She woke up in the middle of her nightmares again, muscles tense and aching. Feeling guilty for waking Ariel the night before, she didn't want to repeat that by crying again— so she held in her pain.

Binny was wide awake and curled up in an anxious ball at the corner of the bed when Ariel woke up the next morning. Ariel gave Binny a penetrating look, and Binny knew she could see the state she was in.

Putting a smile on her face, Ariel skipped her morning shower, pulled on her overalls and with a cheerful voice, asked, "How about visiting Polly before breakfast? Maybe her eggs have hatched."

Binny merely started grooming herself.

"Binny?" Ariel said.

Binny continued to groom herself.

"Come on, Binny," Ariel murmured. "You can't help your baby by overstressing. Let's go get some fresh air."

Binny sighed deeply. "My baby is a fish, Ariel. Do you not see? My favorite food is also fish. I feel like a monster."

Ariel put her hands on her hips. "Don't be ridiculous. You love your baby. And whether or not she is a fish, you will continue to love her. Now, stop what you are doing and follow me."

"How can I control my instincts, Ariel? You know the frog and scorpion story," she said and went on to explain when Ariel looked mystified. "A scorpion bites the frog that's helping her cross the river and says, 'I couldn't help it, it's in my nature.' And they both died."

"Nonsense. First of all, you are not like a scorpion. You are a caring, kind cat. By the way, canned fish food for cats is not part of your natural diet. Your canned fish is filled with all sorts of unnecessary things that are not fish, and could be hazardous to your health," Ariel added.

Binny's mouth watered, imagining a big seafood dinner. "Those fish dinners are delicious, Ariel." Wracked with guilt, her eyes welled up with tears.

Ariel shrugged. "Because they add so many things to your hodgepodge of canned fish to make it delightful. You are more mature and smarter. Stop pitying yourself. We're going out." She walked out the door. "I have an idea," she called over her shoulder.

Binny thought for a moment before finally getting up to follow. "You know, you're right," she said, not knowing whether Ariel could hear her or not. "It's weird, isn't it? Fish or not, that baby is mine, and I'm her loving mother."

Chapter 16

SUNLIGHT WAS DANCING on the magnolia tree's pinkish-white flowers, an open invitation to the bees.

Ariel looked carefully to spot Polly. "Where is her nest?"

Binny leaped onto a branch close to the ground and climbed. "I found her, Ariel," she called out after a moment. "Hey, Polly! Did your babies hatch yet?"

"No, but any time, now."

Ariel's face brightened to a smile. "Congratulations, Polly. Happy egg-sitting."

"How is Moon Girl doing?" Polly chirped.

Binny twitched her tail, growled a depressed meow, and scuffled her paws. "My girl is not well. Dr. Andreas says she is some kind of fish."

"No, way!" Polly screeched, flapping her wings in astonishment. "What nonsense. I have never heard of a fish living on land."

"Me, either. But Ariel says anything's possible," Binny muttered, giving a slight groan.

"We came to ask you if you could help us to call Cleo for a meeting. But I can see you are very busy," Ariel said.

"That is true, but I think I can still help you." Polly then called to Bertha the robin, who had just landed on a nearby branch.

"Hello, Bertha," Polly greeted. "Binny wants to talk to Cleo. Can you send a message to her?"

Bertha tilted her dark head left, right, then forward. "I landed to watch and listen for the sound of earthworms before the day gets too warm, dear. But I will gladly deliver Binny's message to Cleo." She tucked her head and opened her dark gray wings, displaying her reddish-maroon breast, and flew away, caroling, "No worries. I'll be there in a minute."

Walking back and forth, Binny waited impatiently for Cleo at the front porch. She was alert, listening to every noise. She gulped the warm, sticky air into her lungs, wishing all of this could be washed away with a rainstorm.

Breathing heavily, Cleo finally appeared at the gate in the afternoon.

"Sorry I could not get here earlier. But I have good news for you. Your baby girl is fine."

Binny wiggled her tail and rubbed Cleo's nose with one paw. "Oh, thank you, my dear friend. Now tell me everything, please."

"I saw her leap from her container with a splash, right onto the doc's desk. She glowed again last night. You should have seen Doc's face when *that* happened," Cleo said with a gruff, growly chuckle. "He immediately called his friend, an expert in marine life. They talked for hours! He even sent photos of Moon Girl. I heard him say 'crossover species,' although I don't know what it means. But don't worry, Binny. I'm guessing that you will see Moon Girl in the next day or two."

Binny dropped her head in disappointment, digging her claws into the ground. "I don't know if I can keep my sanity for the next day or two, Cleo."

Cleo put her paws to Binny's face and rubbed her nose softly. "Keep your hopes high. You are a strong lady."

"It is research. That's why it takes longer than a regular office visit," Ariel said to Binny when she shared her conversation with Cleo.

Binny groaned. "Why can't I see her?"

Ariel embraced Binny and softly brushed her prickly pelt with her fingers. "I don't see why you shouldn't be able to see her. It would be good for both of you. Let me call him."

Binny stood up and gave Ariel a kiss to thank her. Ariel picked her up and walked to the living room to call Dr. Andreas. After she hung up the phone, she smiled at Binny. "We have an appointment for tomorrow, first thing in the morning."

Binny moved her whiskers forward, stretched her head up, and gazed into Ariel's eyes, feeling a sparkle of hope. "I wish I could take her home tomorrow, Ariel. I . . . I don't know why, but I still don't trust him."

Ariel stared into Binny's emerald eyes. "No one is going to take Moon Girl away from you, Binny."

Binny stayed upright, her heart pounding, all night. She ran in circles around Ariel's bedroom until she threw herself down in exhaustion next to the bed. She wriggled on her tummy and bit her paws compulsively. In her half-sleep, she dreamed of being able to bring Moon Girl home the next day. The following morning, Binny, panting heavily, her nostrils flaring, had her emerald eyes fixed on Ariel's sleeping face.

Ariel opened her eyes and smiled. "Good morning, dear. I know—I can't wait to see Moon Girl, either."

They both tiptoed down the stairs to avoid waking Mrs. Cobbler.

At the front porch, Ariel picked Binny up. "Your legs must be exhausted from pacing around all night."

Binny objected but Ariel carried her all the way to Dr. Andreas's office. The crisp breeze refreshed their spirits, cleared their worries. Their noses filled with the scent of blossoming spring flowers, warming their hearts.

"Even the Earth is on our side," Ariel said with a chuckle.

They arrived at the clinic, and Ariel knocked on the door. "Thanks for letting us see Moon Girl, Doc," she said when Dr. Andreas welcomed them in.

"Come on in, Ariel. I wanted to ask you a couple of questions about your pet. Where did you find it?"

"Not me, Doc. Binny found her. She told me that the screech owl, Adel, saw her fall from the sky."

He lifted his eyebrows. "Ah, I see. I'll tell you what—how about we skip the 'I can understand the animals' game?"

Ariel glanced at Binny and whispered, "Don't panic. We don't have to prove anything to him." She turned back to Dr. Andreas. "How is she doing? Can we see her, please?"

Dr. Andreas slowly nodded. "You may, of course. But I can't discharge your pet today."

Binny's heart sank as he walked out of the room.

After a moment, Dr. Andreas returned, holding the glass bowl. "Here it is, safe and sound."

As soon as he placed the bowl on his desk, Binny jumped up to see her. There she was, lying still on her red sand.

Binny meowed softly, "I miss you so much."

Recognizing her mama's voice, Moon Girl raised her upper body, giggled, and flung herself out of the water toward Binny. With a motherly instinct, she nuzzled Moon Girl gently before dropping her back in her bowl.

Ariel faced Dr. Andreas. "Thanks so much, Doctor. But it looks like your patient is well. Could you please release her today?"

Dr. Andreas sighed, picking up the bowl. "Ariel, she is an unusual case. My friend and I haven't completed our research yet. We're at the edge of a breakthrough, though."

Ariel's face turned pale as Binny yowled.

Binny placed her paws on Ariel's leg. "Please—please don't let the doctor take my baby!" Ariel's face turned red and Binny knew it was with the realization that believing Dr. Andreas was a big mistake, that she had endangered Moon Girl's life.

"Breakthrough?" Ariel asked with a tremble in her voice. "What do you mean? You aren't saying that we can't have her back at all, are you?"

Ignoring her distress, Dr. Andreas just shrugged. "It is too early to answer your questions. Please be patient and wait a couple of days. We're getting closer."

Her lip quivered. "Closer to what?"

Without replying, Dr. Andreas turned away and walked to the door with the bowl.

Moon Girl glowed with one long and two short flashes, then the door shut and the light was gone. Binny remembered her nightmare—so similar to what was happening now. She hissed fiercely, leaped at the door, and crashed into the doorknob.

Yowling in pain, she cried, "What should we do?"

Ariel and Cleo stared at each other, shivering in dismay. A bone-chilling silence settled in the room. Cleo rolled her eyes, twitching her ears as she padded over to Binny. She nuzzled her, devastated by the broken trust in her master.

Ariel stamped her foot. "I didn't see this coming." She knelt to smooth Binny's spiky fur.

Binny groaned in utter desolation.

Ariel turned to peer into Cleo's eyes. "You are our ears, now. Be his shadow. We must learn about his plans."

"What? Why me?" Cleo growled, stepping away from her.

Ariel lifted Cleo's muzzle. "It has to be you, Cleo. You must make your choice, right now. It's either your owner or us."

Cleo whined and looked at Binny, and Binny knew she felt uneasy betraying her master, even though Dr. Andreas had broken her trust. "Why can't it be both? Binny, please say something."

After a long moment, Binny nodded. "Please, Cleo." She quietly followed Ariel out of the building, thinking that things were going south very quickly.

On the way home, Ariel turned to Binny and asked, "Do you think Cleo will be on our side, Binny?"

"Of course, she will help us. She is a member of our organization. And she is my best friend," she added.

"Let's hope so," Ariel said. "You really never know who your friends are unless you've been through rough times . . . because you can't trust a person who says they are your best friend only in good times. You know who is a real friend if they stick around in difficult times."

"How can you live without trusting anyone, Ariel?" Binny chided. "Being suspicious is not the right way to live your life. You have to have faith in your friends. Disbelieving is the road to misery."

Chapter 17

BINNY HAD YET another sleepless night.

As soon as she closed her eyes, her breathing became harder, and her body felt like it had broken into bits and pieces. She played the memory, over and over in her mind, of Moon Girl leaping out of her bowl toward her. Then, her last glow, when the doctor had taken her from the room. *Is my baby hungry? Is she sleeping well?* Her thoughts swirled and whirled in her head until the wee hours of the morning.

She rolled onto her belly and gazed at Ariel's face, listening to her steady breathing. She was in a deep sleep. *I can't wait any longer for her to wake up*, she thought and tiptoed downstairs.

Once she was outside, the sky began to lighten, and an orange-tinged fog drifted around Binny's body. Her paws became damp as she padded past Ripley Street, and at one point, she stumbled as she shifted her weight to her strong leg. She narrowed her eyes and glanced around in mortification; luckily, no one was there to see her misstep. Everyone was asleep, sailing through their dreams. She limped uphill through the slowly rising fog.

Binny was panting heavily by the time she reached Dr. Andreas's house. She crouched down and stared up at the doctor's bedroom, hoping Cleo would be there. Spotting a tree branch close to the bedroom window, she jumped and landed on it. She peered through the glass and saw Cleo stretched out on the floor beside the bed, her head now lifted and ears erect. Binny gave the sill a soft pat, and Cleo's head jerked toward her. When she saw who it was, she quietly got up and met Binny outside, looking sleep-deprived.

"What's up? You shouldn't be here. It is too risky."

"I can't sleep. How is my baby doing?"

Cleo rubbed her eyes. "Moon Girl is fine. I was planning to come to your place today. I think the Doc made his decision, and he's going to call Ariel."

Binny gazed at her with hope. "Can I keep my baby?"

"I don't know, Binny," Cleo said. "There were too many medical words in his conversation. C'mon. Let me walk you home. Today will be a big day. You need to rest."

For a moment, Binny stared at Cleo, wriggling her tail with frustration. But finally, she let her escort her home as the sun cleared the horizon.

Once home, Binny scurried up to Ariel's bedroom, pounced onto the girl's bed, and licked her face. "Dr. Andreas is going to call you today, Ariel," she announced as Ariel rubbed her eyes. "He's made his decision."

They exchanged glances, knowing they'd never fall back asleep. "How about a little research, then, to kill time?" Ariel said, sitting up. She stretched, stood, and went to her desk, Binny following at her heels.

With Binny watching her every move, Ariel meticulously searched the internet for any kind of fish that could live on land until her eyes were seeing double.

"Nothing," she said.

Binny hopped down from the desk, thinking hard. "Look for small fish that were forced to live on land before we existed," she meowed after a moment.

"Like . . . dinosaurs?" Ariel asked, brow furrowed, and then her eyes lit up. "Hey, you could be on to something. There are plenty of fish in the ocean that have survived since prehistoric times. Hagfish, sturgeon, sawfish . . . we learned about them in school. But"—her face shadowed with thought again—"I don't think Moon Girl is one of them."

When Dr. Andreas finally called Ariel, both she and Binny were on the verge of collapsing with anxiety and exhaustion. After hanging up the phone, Ariel turned to Binny. "We have to go see the Doc again. But how do you propose we leave the house without Auntie noticing our disappearance?"

"I don't know. But you have to figure out the most convincing excuse. And please don't say that I am sick again—unless you want your auntie to tag along."

Ariel paced the room. "I feel guilty for deceiving her. And if Dr. Andreas won't discharge Moon Girl today, we'll need Auntie's intervention, no matter what—we'd have to tell her. But for now, how about I call one of Auntie's friends over for tea. We could disappear for an hour and she shouldn't notice."

Binny nodded in agreement.

Ariel called Jenn for an afternoon tea, telling her aunt that a visitor was on the way. "I thought you needed company, so I invited Ms. Jenn. She likes your blueberry muffins. They will go great with your Earl Grey tea," she added with a hopeful smile.

Mrs. Cobbler returned the smile, delighted, and then hurried to the kitchen to start baking.

Later, once the ladies had settled in the living room with tea and muffins, Ariel scooped Binny up in her arms. "Let's go." At the front porch, a perfumed breeze kissed their faces. White, patchy clouds shifted in the sparkling blue sky, raising their hopes. "Even Earth has good vibes for us. We'll have Moon Girl today, Binny."

Binny softly meowed in reply.

Ariel kept her head down to avoid familiar faces as they scurried toward Main Street. When they stepped into Dr. Andreas's office, he was on the phone.

"We must pursue the case. There is more research that needs to be done," he added before hanging up and turning to Ariel and Binny.

Ariel swallowed hard. "You have good news for us?"

Cleo trotted over and stood next to Binny. She seemed to be on edge.

Dr. Andreas gave them a smile that made Binny's fur stand up, and his eyes seemed to sparkle with greedy hunger. "Please sit down, Ariel. Yes, I have news for you. My friend, Dr. Rich, searched some scientific books and sent photos to the marine experts. We're close to publishing our research." He rubbed his hands together. "We—"

"Meaning?" Ariel said.

"We are making a breakthrough discovery. Your pet is a crossover species—a mix of Pacific leaping blenny and a bio-fluorescence species—although we have not yet identified the exact type of glowing organism. It could be either a dinoflagellate or some type of glowing marine plankton. We need to experiment further to prove our research to the scientific community."

"My girl is not a science experiment," Binny whispered fiercely to Ariel. She panted heavily, feeling that the worst was yet to come.

Ariel scrunched up her face. "What is a . . . a Pacific leaping blenny? And if it's a fish, how can it survive out of the sea?"

Dr. Andreas steepled his fingers like a professor. "It is similar to a mudskipper and can survive out of the water for several hours because it breathes through its skin. It leaps around the tidal rocky areas where they live in holes. The leaping blenny may prove humankind's evolution from the sea to the land. But since they need to keep their skin and gills moist, they can never be too far from the water, or they will suffocate. I believe your pet blenny got sick because of a lack of the right kind of moisture."

"But, " Ariel said, her forehead creasing further, "how did she get here? Can the Pacific leaping blenny fly?"

"No, it can't fly. But Dr. Rich and I came up with a theory. First of all, the red sand is scarce and iron rich. The mixture your pet was wrapped in is Alaea salt and sand. The only place that harvests this red salt using traditional methods is Kauai. When the sun evaporates the seawater from manmade salt ponds, the salt is harvested from the bottom. It is then mixed with red dirt— called Alaea—before being transferred into a basket."

Ariel nibbled her bottom lip as Binny angrily rubbed against her leg. "But what was a blenny doing in a salt pond?"

Dr. Andreas sighed, looking at his watch. "Your pet was probably accidentally picked up by folks collecting ocean water or sand to build salt ponds. The blenny is very small, hard to notice. Who knows—it may not have been the only one stranded in the salt ponds. Its entire family might have been, as well."

Ariel shook her head slowly. "How could Moon Girl possibly have traveled from Kauai to Nauvoo, Illinois, though?"

Binny yowled. "This is ridiculous! You don't believe him, do you, Ariel?"

Cleo hurried over to press her muzzle to Binny's face. "What he's said so far is true, my friend. I may not have understood many of the medical words when he and his friend were talking, but all of this he is telling you now? It is as he says."

Dr. Andreas glanced over at Binny's shaking form and then looked back at Ariel. "Our life depends on nature's miracles, Ariel. Perhaps the basket of damp salt holding your pet ended up in a market, and maybe a customer offered to use their own leather bag to wrap it in. And then maybe—just maybe—a tropical storm or monsoon struck the island, and this little basket of salt wrapped in a leather bag somehow got caught up in it. The wind could have sent your pet into the atmosphere. And she landed here." He shrugged. "The moisture in the leather bag finally dried out, and the blenny became ill. And you found it. See? Miracles of nature."

Binny yowled again, her tail twisted with fury. "Of course, it's a miracle. Now, let's take Moon Girl and go. My gut tells me this won't end well for us."

Ariel nodded, clapping her hands together. "Well, again, thanks for your search, Doc. But we'll be taking Moon Girl home now."

Dr. Andreas's expression darkened. "We haven't researched how it produces light, yet."

Ariel's face turned pale. "You said it was something to do with plankton and dinoflagellate, right? So, yeah—thanks for explaining it all to us. But now you can continue your work without her, right?"

"Ariel," Dr. Andreas said, taking a deep breath and glowering, "your pet is now in the hands of science. You can have another pet. Send my regards to your aunt, Mrs. Cobbler. You can leave now."

A shocked silence filled the room, and Ariel's eyes filled with tears. Clenching her fists and grinding her teeth, she put her hands on her hips as Binny growled by her side. "You can't have her, Dr. Andreas. Moon Girl belongs to us."

Doctor Andreas raised his eyebrows. "Don't make me call your aunt about breaking into my office," he said, his voice low and threatening.

Ariel's body shook with sobs. Binny snarled at Dr. Andreas, staggering forward, but at the last moment, she stopped herself, knowing there was nothing they could do. Whipping her tail across Ariel's legs, she growled, "We have to leave. Now."

Leaving Moon Girl behind was Binny's worst nightmare, and she could hardly hold herself upright. Collapsing onto the cobblestones once she and Ariel were outside, she mewed piteously up at her. "What can we do?"

Ariel's tear-filled eyes were lowered, her cheeks flushed with guilt. "Taking her here is all my fault. We'll break in tonight and get Moon Girl. Send a message to Cleo, asking for her help."

Binny crouched on the ground, cooling down her burning belly, and she gazed up at Ariel with love and relief. "I'm so glad to have a friend like you." She sighed.

Chapter 18

"CLEO WILL RESCUE Moon Girl from Dr. Andreas' protected area tonight," Binny told Ariel later that day. "She asked me to wait by the maple tree. I have high hopes about our plan to save her."

"That's wonderful news," Ariel said, clapping her hands, but then her smile dimmed. "But I don't think our basement is a safe place for Moon Girl, anymore. When Dr. Andreas realizes what we did, he'll call the police and they'll find her for sure. Who can help us find a safer place, Binny?"

Binny's stomach did a little flip. "Maybe Missy can help."

"Great. Go talk to Missy before dinner," Ariel said. "My brain can't keep up anymore—I need a nap."

The pouring rain and crashing thunder that night made the walk to Dr. Andreas's clinic a nightmare. Both Binny and Ariel were soaking wet when they met Cleo.

Ariel handed Moon Girl's empty basket over to Cleo. "Be careful," she whispered with a shaky voice.

Cleo took the basket in her teeth, wagged her tail as a reply, and then crept back through the open window into the doctor's office.

They both tensed up while waiting for Cleo. Their hearts were pounding, but they tried not to show it on their faces as the storm raged around them. After what seemed like hours, Ariel and Binny breathed twin sighs of relief when Cleo appeared with Moon Girl's basket in her mouth.

Cleo handed it to Binny. "I'm sorry it took so long; Moon Girl was in a well-protected area, and I had to avoid the cameras while moving her. She is safe in her container with water. Now, go—quickly."

Ariel took the basket, and they ran from shadow to shadow, avoiding streetlights, Moon Girl burbling happily all the while.

Binny panted deeply. "How far away is Missy's home?"

Ariel sighed. "I'm afraid we can't make it tonight, Binny. It's not safe to walk that far in this mess—we'll be lucky if we can make it home without being struck by lightning. We'll go first thing in the morning. I promise."

Binny knew she was right but was devastated nonetheless.

A while later, as Ariel eased open the front door, she asked, "Do you think Cleo was able to avoid the clinic's cameras?"

"Hopefully—but we might have a serious problem explaining this to your auntie if we track mud and water inside the house," Binny meowed.

Ariel took a deep breath. "That is the least of my worries."

She turned on her flashlight and tiptoed up the stairs. Binny padded up by her side watched Ariel place the basket behind the nightstand.

"This will all be over tomorrow," she meowed quietly, and after Ariel dried Binny's fur with a soft towel, they both slept deeply.

After what seemed like only minutes, the doorbell woke them. Binny and Ariel sat bolt upright as a man's voice drifted up the stairs.

"Good morning, Mrs. Cobbler."

"Oh! Good morning, Officer McNamara," Mrs. Cobbler said, sounding discombobulated. Ariel swallowed back a yelp of alarm.

"What can I do for you?" Mrs. Cobbler asked.

"I'm sorry to bother you, but it seems that Dr. Andreas filed a report against your niece," he said, sounding uncomfortable.

"He—he *what?*"

Ariel stared at Binny with wide eyes for a moment before they silently crept out of bed, down the hall, and to the top of the stairway. They peered downstairs, where Mrs. Cobbler stood with her hands on her hips, seemingly at a loss for words.

Officer McNamara cast his eyes about, looking like he wished to be anywhere else. "Yes, Mrs. Cobbler, ma'am. He claims that Ariel stole a valuable fish from his office. I have a warrant to search your house." He shuffled his feet as he pulled out a piece of paper.

"My—*my* niece? Ariel would never steal anything—a fish from his office, you say?" Mrs. Cobbler sputtered, shaking her head in disbelief.

Officer McNamara shrugged and looked helpless in the face of Mrs. Cobbler's distress. "I'm sorry, ma'am. I'm just following orders."

Mrs. Cobbler stepped back and lifted her head. "That is a serious accusation."

The officer handed over the warrant paper. "Please cooperate, Mrs. Cobbler."

Mrs. Cobbler scrutinized it. "This is crazy. And, of course, you can come in. We always obey the law."

"Thank you, ma'am. I'm sure it is all just a misunderstanding," he added, following Mrs. Cobbler to the living room.

Ariel gave Binny an agonized glance as Mrs. Cobbler called her to come to the living room.

In her pajamas, Ariel slowly made her way downstairs and stood next to her aunt.

"This is officer McNamara, Ariel," Mrs. Cobbler said, peering into Ariel's face. "Dr. Andreas has filed a complaint. He alleges that you stole a valuable fish from his office."

"*What?*" Ariel gasped, trying to buy some time as her thoughts whirled in her head.

"Dr. Andreas reported that he caught you and your cat breaking into his office," Officer McNamara said gently. "He also said you were both at the clinic more than twice this week to talk about the fish."

Mrs. Cobbler raised her brows and looked at her niece. "You said you took Binny to the doctor's office because she wasn't feeling well. I know nothing about you stealing from his office." She leaned closer, her eyes worried. "Is it true, Ariel?"

Ariel let the air out from her lungs in a whoosh as her mind went utterly blank for a moment. And then, she knew what she had to do. Clearing her throat and squaring her shoulders, she looked her aunt in the eye. "Yes, Auntie. We visited the doctor's office. But we did not steal from him." Her breath hitched with the beginning of tears.

"Don't panic," Binny mewed by her side. "*We're* not the thieves. *He* is!"

Mrs. Cobbler gave her niece a little smile. "I trust my niece, officer. And I am guessing you were right—there is a misunderstanding."

Officer McNamara sized them up. "Very well, then. You don't have to worry. Let me do my job."

He strolled to the kitchen and checked inside the cabinets. Then he inspected the living room, looking around and under all the furniture. "It is clear. I would like to check the rooms on the top floor."

"Follow me," Mrs. Cobbler said, walking toward the staircase to guide Officer McNamara.

"Please, officer, don't look into my room," Ariel said in a squeaky voice. It's . . . uh, messy."

Mrs. Cobbler smiled. "It is okay, Ariel. He's not looking for cleanliness."

Ariel's blood rushed to her head as Officer McNamara and Mrs. Cobbler headed upstairs. "We're caught, Binny. I'll take full responsibility."

"Calm down, Ariel. I already took care of it," she meowed.

Ariel sat on the floor next to Binny and caressed her fur gently. "Oh, thank goodness. Is she in the basement? I'm so sorry, Binny—it was a terrible idea to ask Dr. Andreas for help. This is all my fault." She had tears in her eyes.

"Nonsense. You tried to save my baby. Besides, my girl is—"

Officer McNamara and Mrs. Cobbler came back downstairs.

"Have I seen the entire house, ma'am?"

"Well, I have basement access from the kitchen. Just storage for my memorabilia. You're welcome to check it out, but I'm afraid I can't manage those steep stairs anymore," Mrs. Cobbler said with a sigh.

He gave her a nod and headed to the basement.

"I'll be arrested any minute, now," Ariel whispered, her voice quavering. "I'll miss you, Binny."

"Don't panic, Ariel," Binny whispered. "All will be well."

Mrs. Cobbler shook her head. "When this is over, you both have some explaining to do."

Ariel's cheeks turn red, and she looked at the floor to hide her tears. Binny stood in front of Ariel, raised her tail, and stretched her front paws. "Blame me. I don't want you to get into the trouble."

Officer McNamara re-entered, smiling. "Nothing suspicious.

Ariel's jaw fell open.

"The allegations will have to be dropped. Thank you again for your cooperation." He smiled again and gave them a salute. "Have a good day, everyone."

Mrs. Cobbler smiled back at the officer, closed the door behind him, turned around, and crossed her arms. "In the living room. *Now*."

Chapter 19

"SILLY ME," ARIEL whispered to Binny on their way into the living room to meet their fate. "No one could possibly find *anything* in Auntie's jumbled basement. Good job, Binny."

"He didn't find her because she is not in the basement, Ariel," Binny said, and then chuckled at Ariel's astounded expression. "I woke up last night, anxious that someone might show up in the morning, so I took action. She is in Missy's backyard house. But she can't stay there forever."

Ariel took a deep breath and blew it out. "You should have told me that before. I almost had a heart attack. But the worst is still yet to come. Wish me luck talking to Auntie."

"I'll be right beside you," Binny said, although she dragged her paws as she followed Ariel to the living room. Mrs. Cobbler was in her favorite Queen Anne chair, her arms still crossed. "So?"

Binny looked up at her two dearest human friends; Ariel was doing her best not to cry, wringing her hands and biting her lip. Mrs. Cobbler was gazing at her niece, and Binny could see the woman was struggling to keep a firm expression on her face—and losing.

The angry lines on Mrs. Cobbler's face softened. "You know I'm here to help. Please tell me what's going on. Is there a problem?"

"A problem? Oh, Auntie . . . it's much more than that," Ariel said, looking as though she felt dizzy, and she raised her hands to clutch her face. "You have to believe us, Auntie. We just wanted to save Moon Girl."

Mrs. Cobbler's eyebrows shot up.

"Binny's child."

Mrs. Cobbler folded her hands carefully. "You know Binny can't have babies, Ariel." She studied her closely. "Are you okay, dear?"

Ariel gave a shuddering sigh. "Yes, Auntie. I'm fine—I'm just really, really worried." Tears spilling down her cheeks, and she tried to wipe them away.

Mrs. Cobbler stood up and sat next to Ariel. She wiped her face tenderly, she then held her wet hands. "Well, I'm worried about *you*. None of this makes sense."

"Please, believe me, Auntie. Binny adopted a thing that came from the sky. Then her baby got sick. We sneaked into the Doc's office to find a cure in his medical books and got caught," Ariel said.

Mrs. Cobbler gasped. "You *did* break in?"

Binny whispered, "I started this. Tell her the truth, Ariel."

"Shh. Let me handle it," Ariel muttered and then turned back to Mrs. Cobbler. "Please let me explain."

Mrs. Cobbler nodded after a moment.

"At first, Dr. Andreas didn't believe me—same as you, now. Then, once he saw her, he agreed to cure her. But I guess what Binny had actually adopted was a rare, glowing fish. Dr. Andreas wouldn't give Moon Girl back after he examined her. He wanted to own her as a science experiment."

Mrs. Cobbler's eyes grew wider and wider. "And then?"

"When he refused to return Binny's baby, Cleo brought her to us, and we hid Moon Girl in a safe place. We are not criminals, Auntie! We were just protecting her." Tears streamed down Ariel's face again. "Can you help us save Moon Girl?"

Mrs. Cobbler gave Ariel a look of dismay. "This isn't exactly how I thought you'd be spending your visit. I'm trying to digest your story, but it is hard to believe, Ariel."

Binny rubbed up against Ariel's leg as she wiped her tears with her sleeve. Her face was hot and puffy. "Please, please, trust me, Auntie. You are the only person now who can save Moon Girl."

Binny jumped into Mrs. Cobbler's arms and stared into her eyes. "Don't punish Ariel, please," she mewed and yowled. "It was all my fault."

Mrs. Cobbler felt Binny's trembling body under the prickle of her pelt, and she hugged her. She then tenderly wiped Ariel's cheek. "Oh, my sweet babies, don't cry. No matter what, I'll always help you."

She put Binny down and paced around the room. Ariel and Binny watched wordlessly, and it seemed to take a thousand tail lengths for Mrs. Cobbler to finally speak. "I'd like to see Moon Girl. After that, we can discuss what to do to protect her. Where is she now?"

"Oh, thank you, thank you, Auntie," Ariel shrieked, clapping. "She is in Missy's backyard house."

Mrs. Cobbler raised her brows. "Is that Binny's adorable friend who visits me?"

"Yes, Auntie. Missy is Ms. Jenn's cat. I know your friend is very kind to us, but please don't tell her our secret," Ariel said.

"Of course, dear. I'll call Jenn and plan a visit. Wash your face and put a proper dress on."

In a matter of time, Mrs. Cobbler and Ariel were ready. Despite her knee pain, Mrs. Cobbler walked briskly, and Ariel and Binny worriedly followed her, praying she would agree to help Moon Girl.

Ms. Jenn greeted them at the door. "What a pleasant surprise to get your call. Join me for afternoon tea—I baked your favorite apple pie," she added. "Good to see you again, Ariel. And thanks for bringing Binny, too. My Missy will enjoy the company."

Mrs. Cobbler smiled. "Thank you, Jenn, for accepting our visit on such short notice. Can we sit in your beautiful garden?"

"Certainly, dear," Ms. Jenn replied, blushing with pride, and turned to lead them to the backyard.

The yard was fenced by green velvet boxwood, and the sunny side of the garden was filled with blooming beauties of pink, white, and purple spring flowerbeds—tulips, narcissus, and hyacinth—accompanying the red, white, and purple roses that were ready to bloom. In the middle area, there was an antique-looking pedestal birdbath alongside a raised vegetable and herb garden.

"Oh!" Mrs. Cobbler exclaimed, looking around, and then turned to the shady side of the garden. "All the Blue Angel hostas and creeping vines—look how lovely they are, surrounding Missy's adorable summer house. You've worked so hard, Jenn."

Jenn blushed again. "Well, yes—but gardening makes me happy, Mary. Please make yourselves comfortable. It is a lovely day to be outside."

They settled into cozy, colorful, cushioned chairs. Missy came to greet Binny, meowing, "Your baby is fine—she will be thrilled to see you."

"The doctor is accusing us of stealing her, and we had to confess our secret to Mrs. Cobbler. Can you bring her outside without being seen by Ms. Jenn? If Mrs. Cobbler believes us, I know she will help to rescue my girl," Binny meowed back.

Missy wiggled her tail in excitement. "Hmm. We must divert Ms. Jenn's attention to take her outside. The best place to hide her is under the bed of hostas."

Binny nuzzled her face. "Good plan. Ms. Jenn will be busy serving soon; I'll tell Ariel to bring Mrs. Cobbler to the hostas when Ms. Jenn goes to the kitchen."

Right on schedule, Jenn asked her guests, "How do you drink your tea, dears? Or would you rather have a glass of apple juice, Ariel?"

"Just tea with milk for me, thank you, Jenn," Mrs. Cobbler replied.

"Apple juice is good. Thank you, ma'am," Ariel said.

As soon as Jenn went to the kitchen, Missy raced to her little house to bring Moon Girl to the hostas, and Ariel pointed in that direction. "Moon Girl is there, Auntie. But we must hurry." She stood and followed Binny across the lawn.

Mrs. Cobbler scurried over. "Where is she? I can't—"

Moon Girl leapt out of the water container in the basket and landed at Binny's feet, glowing and giggling joyfully.

"Oh! It is God's miracle, Ariel!" Mrs. Cobbler exclaimed.

"God's miracle?" Jenn said from behind them. "Oh, my, Mary—I don't know about *that*. They're just my happy Blue Angel hostas."

Binny and Missy hissed with panic as Jenn placed her serving tray on the patio table and walked toward them. She proudly gazed around at her plants.

"Th-they . . . oh, y-yes, Jenn," Mrs. Cobbler said. "They are gorgeous, indeed."

Jenn looked toward her birdbath, and Ariel quickly picked up Moon Girl, tucked her into her right palm, and gently cupped her fingers around her.

"Hmm. This is odd. I haven't seen this, before." Jenn picked up the empty basket and turned it over in her hands, frowning.

Mrs. Cobbler cleared her throat and looked down at her hands. "That is . . . um, yes, very odd."

Ariel stepped forward. "It was mine. I gave it to Binny to play with. She must have let Missy have it."

"Well, then," Jenn said with a smile. She put the basket down in front of Missy. "Here, dear. Please keep it at your home. Your tea is getting cold, Mary. Please sit down and enjoy the afternoon sun with me."

While Jenn and Mrs. Cobbler sat down to afternoon tea, Ariel gingerly slid Moon Girl back into the basket. "Keep her safe, Missy."

The rest of the afternoon tea went as usual, except for Mrs. Cobbler's obvious distraction. Binny could see that Ariel was trying very hard to keep her aunt focused, but despite her efforts, Jenn still looked concerned by the time they all left.

Chapter 20

BINNY'S THOUGHTS WERE in a whirl as she stared at Mrs. Cobbler once they were back in their own living room. Mrs. Cobbler hadn't said whether or not she would help save Moon Girl, and Binny was beside herself with anxiety.

She looked up at Ariel. "Do you think Mrs. Cobbler will help?"

Ariel softly stroked Binny's fur. "I'm praying for it."

"I don't understand why it's taking her so long to decide," Binny mewed with a trembling voice.

"It might be a good sign. It means she is still thinking about it," Ariel said.

Mrs. Cobbler sat down in her chair with a gusty sigh. "I'm still shaking. I've witnessed a miracle, Ariel."

"Are you going to help us, Auntie?" Ariel asked.

Mrs. Cobbler shook her head. "I'm afraid not, dear. It is not right."

Binny yowled, "But, why? I found her. She is my baby."

Ariel clasped her hands desperately. "Why can't Binny have her, Auntie? Are you really going to let Dr. Andreas use her for his experiments? It will eventually kill her." Her voice broke.

Mrs. Cobbler shook her head again. "I'm not giving her to Dr. Andreas. But Binny can't keep Moon Girl because she has to return to her natural environment to survive. You told me she got very sick. She was dehydrated."

Binny pounced into Mrs. Cobbler's lap and licked her hands. "Please, please don't take my baby away from me."

Ariel clenched and unclenched her fingers. "Can't you see? It's excruciating for Binny. Her baby will be so sad, too. They love each other, Auntie. Can you please find a way to keep them together?" Tears washed over her cheeks.

"I—"

They were all startled by the doorbell.

Mrs. Cobbler frowned as she scurried to the front door. "I'm not expecting anyone. How very rude."

She opened the door, and to everyone's horror, it was Dr. Andreas. He looked at Mrs. Cobbler from under furrowed brows. "Mrs. Cobbler, please see reason. My discovery is a significant breakthrough. I must have the specimen back to continue my research."

Mrs. Cobbler frowned. "I can't help you, Dr. Andreas. Please leave now."

He narrowed his eyes. "You can't keep it. I must have it back."

Mrs. Cobbler closed the door in his face, peeked out the window, and watched him leave.

"Is he gone?" Ariel asked in a trembling voice.

"Yes, but I'm sure he will be back," Mrs. Cobbler said. Then she saw Binny's twitching body, picked her up, and peered into her fiery emerald eyes. "I'm sorry, Binny. My heart aches for you and Moon Girl. I know you love each other. But the only way to save your baby is to return her to where she belongs. What if she has family there?"

Binny twisted her body out from Mrs. Cobbler's arms and landed next to Ariel. "Please do something, Ariel," she moaned, feeling as though her heart was being torn in two.

"There must be some way to keep them together," Ariel wailed. "*Please*, think of something else, Auntie."

Mrs. Cobbler shook her head sadly. "If Binny loves Moon Girl, she needs to accept what is right for her baby. Sometimes doing the right thing is painful, and we must learn to live with our pain if we're giving up something for the greater good."

Binny's breath came in heaving gulps. "How can she expect a mother to leave her baby, Ariel?" she cried, and Ariel asked the question.

Mrs. Cobbler's face softened. "For a good cause, Binny. Your dear mother, Belle, sacrificed her life to protect you. She gave up all the rest of the time she could have had with you so that you could live."

Binny's entire body sagged as she realized this was true.

"But, Auntie," Ariel interjected. "Dr. Andreas told us Moon Girl somehow traveled from Kauai to Nauvoo. How can we take Moon Girl back to her home?"

"I have some airline miles and savings set aside for a rainy day. I will call your parents to get their permission—it will be my treat to you, dear. I'm so proud of you for taking care of Binny and protecting her baby," she said with a loving smile.

Ariel ran to embrace her aunt. "Thank you, Auntie. Can Binny come with us?"

"Of course, dear. Binny deserves to say a proper goodbye to her baby." She picked Binny up and embraced her once more, whispering, "Sorry, honey, but this is the only way to save your Moon Girl."

Looking into Mrs. Cobbler's eyes, so full of kindness and understanding, Binny suddenly truly felt how loved—how very *unconditionally* loved—she was. For the first time, she understood that this woman, who had raised her like her own child, was far more than her owner or mistress. Binny licked her nose, and meowed. *Thank you, Mom.* Mrs. Cobbler gave her a gentle squeeze before putting her down and then bustling off to the phone.

Ariel's parents were delighted to hear about Mrs. Cobbler's vacation plans and thanked her for her generosity, offering to pay Ariel's way. "Nonsense. I'm not rich, but I'm not poor, either. I can manage this little trip. It was my idea and it'll be my treat."

When she got the green light from Ariel's mother, she didn't waste any time calling her travel agent to book the round trip for the next day from Quad Cities airport, Moulin to Lihue airport, Kauai. After she booked the flights for the next day, Mrs. Cobbler asked Ariel to bring Binny's travel crate from the basement, and then rattled off the plan.

"Our flight is at two in the afternoon, so we should be to the airport by one o'clock. Our limousine will pick us up at ten o'clock, which means we will be stopping by to get Moon Girl from Missy by five past ten. Pack enough things for three days." She started to turn away, but then stopped and looked back at Ariel. "I haven't felt so energized in years," she said quietly. "This reminds me of my last trip to Hawaii with Tom. Oh, how I miss him."

Ariel took her hand.

"I know he would do this very same thing if he were still here," she added, her eyes filling with tears.

They all packed their bags and then settled in for the night. It was a long one for Binny. She flipped and flopped on the bed next to Ariel, thinking about her mom, Belle, who gave up her life for her daughter. Now, it was her turn to save Moon Girl—by giving her up. She mewed in misery.

Ariel curled up closer to her, took Binny in her arms. "This is the only way to save your baby, Binny. Be strong," she whispered.

"I'll miss my Moon Girl terribly, Ariel. I don't know how I will stay sane," she meowed tearfully.

"You'll live proudly, knowing that you rescued your girl, Binny. Just pray that everything will go as planned. No more surprises," she added.

They were having breakfast and the doorbell rang at eight. It was Dr. Andreas.

"What do you want?" Mrs. Cobbler said, hands on her hips.

"You have something that belongs to me," he growled.

Her eyes bored into him. "She is not yours, doctor. You accused my niece of being a thief, and you are not welcome here." She started to close the door.

"Don't make me do something you'll regret, Mrs. Cobbler," he said in a low voice, stepping forward and pushing the door open.

Mrs. Cobbler gasped as he entered the house. She shoved him and yelled to Ariel, "Call 911!"

Dr. Andreas panicked and ran to his car. He backed into the street and screeched away—but Binny suspected he hadn't gone far.

Apparently, Mrs. Cobbler felt the same. "He'll probably be watching us from his car, up the street." She turned to Ariel. "Get your bags."

The airport limo arrived, and the driver loaded their luggage into the trunk. Mrs. Cobbler asked the driver to stop by Jenn's place; while Mrs. Cobbler said goodbye to her friend and asked her to water her plants, Ariel would get Moon Girl from Missy's house. It was an excellent plan, and they executed it well.

On the way to the Airport, Binny cuddled Moon Girl's container, and whispered, "Soon you will be home. Mom will always love you, Moon Girl."

All seemed well until the driver looked in his rearview mirror. "There is a black Corolla following behind us. It's been there since we left your house, ma'am. Were you expecting someone to meet up with you at the airport?"

Mrs. Cobbler looked back at the car. "Oh, him—that's just, um . . . a lay-about relative of mine, looking for a handout. Please drive a bit faster, if you don't mind. You just don't know what to expect from folks these days."

"Thankfully, I did online check-in," she murmured to Ariel, "and all our luggage is carry-on." She called their departure gate and requested that a wheelchair be waiting for them on the curbside, and then she asked the driver one more time to increase the speed.

Ariel's face turned white. "Are we going to make it, Auntie?" Binny hissed.

Mrs. Cobbler took Ariel's cold hands. "Of course, dear. Trust your Auntie."

A few minutes later, they pulled up to the curb, where the wheelchair was waiting for them, and with the help of a Ground

Transportation assistant, they made their way to the security checkpoint.

Just then, Dr. Andreas came sprinting in the doors, his car parked illegally outside and a security guard hot on his heels. "Sir! Last warning—stop where you are!" When Dr. Andreas ignored him, the guard keyed his radio. "We have a situation at Gate 1B," the officer yelled into the handset as he pulled out his gun and broke into a sprint after the doctor. "Stop! Hands up, now!"

As Ariel, Mrs. Cobbler, and Binny looked on from the security gate, agog, Dr. Andreas stumbled to a stop with raised arms. The security officer searched him and read him his rights as he handcuffed him.

Mrs. Cobbler sighed and smiled at Ariel who was holding Binny's travel bag. "I hope they lock him up until we finish our mission, dear."

Binny hugged Moon Girl tightly. "You are safe, my baby," she whispered, her heart both overflowing with love and breaking and the same time. "We're taking you home."

Chapter 21

CHILLY AIR FUNNELED through Binny's pelt. Its whirling gusts squeezed her body into a furball. "You must be strong!" It was her mom, Belle's voice. Her pelt prickled from her spine. She strengthened herself with a sharp tingling and watched her front paws transform into wings. She swayed in the whirling air, away from Dr. Andreas's rumbling order. "Stop! Return Moon Girl to me!"

The fluffy clouds blackened and clumped around her. Numbed by the cold air, Binny watched shimmering fog swirl around her seemingly-useless wings, sucked in by the wind tunnel. Time seemed to stand still . . . Until a sudden pull yanked Binny down with almighty speed. The tunnel changed its shape from a horizontal spiral to a vertical funnel before gradually expanding and opening up. Feeling a rapid drop, she yowled fiercely.

"We landed, Binny."

"I had an awful nightmare, Ariel."

Binny gently licked Moon Girl to check if she was dehydrated. Feeling lightheaded asked, "Where are we, Ariel?"

"Kauai. As soon as we drop off our luggage at the hotel, we'll go to Salt Pond Beach to release Moon Girl."

Binny howled with sorrow and curled deeper into the bag. Ariel took her out into her arms and gazed at her emerald eyes, "We must do this to save her."

BINNY HAD NEVER been in such a crowded place before with people rushing all over the place. She followed them closely as they made their way outside to find a taxi to take them to their hotel at Hanapepe Beach. She had to ask Ariel. "Where are we?" many times.

Each time Ariel replied to her, "No worries, Binny. Everything is going well as we planned."

Still, Binny worried about Dr. Andreas following them to steal Moon Girl.

But as her Mom told her, she must not pity herself, and she needed to control Moon Girl's glowing so as not to attract the driver's attention. She whispered to her, "Please be quiet. You will be safe soon."

After more than a thousand whisker twitches, Binny's ears pinned back. "Less than ten minutes ride after dropping off your luggage, Ma'am."

She dipped her head and sniffed Moon Girl's musty odor into her lungs. She softly meowed, "You will always be with me, no matter if we are far apart, my dear girl."

In response, Moon girl gave her one long, and two short glows.

A little later, the back of her throat burned with salty wind, and her eyes opened like two giant balls.

"There is a rocky shore. It's perfect, a safe place for Moon Girl away from beach goers," Mary said to Ariel as she pointed to one side of the beach.

Ariel unzipped Binny's Bag and gently lifted Moon Girl out of the container. "Come over, Binny. It is time to say goodbye to your girl."

Binny dragged her stiff legs toward the rocky ground and looked sorrowfully at her surroundings. Ariel put Moon Girl next to Binny. "What you are doing is noble. Saving your girl's life. Binny. You should be proud of yourself."

Binny retracted her claws to stand still and whimpered sadly, then she sniffed and licked Moon Girl. "Go find your family! I will always love and miss you, my Moon Girl."

She sadly watched Moon Girl disappear under the high tide.

EXCEPT FOR ONE or two break-ins by outsiders, Nauvoo residents and the Friendly Pets Club lived in harmony. One sorrowful heart in the town was Binny. She passed her long days, remembering Moon Girl.

Near the end of her spring break, Ariel picked Binny up and hugged her with excitement. "You don't have to worry about Moon Girl at all. *Strange Creatures* filmed a spotted glowing curious creature at Salt Pond Beach. They reported a glowing Pacific blenny. She is your Moon Girl."

Binny took a relieved breath and cuddled against Ariel.

"Thank you, Ariel," she meowed. "I'm glad you're safe and happy. You'll always be my Moon Girl."

R. Y. Suben is a retired engineer who lives in Chicago, Illinois, with her family. She is a distinguished member of the International Society of Poets. A potpourri of her poem *One Piece* published in 2017. Her children's book T*he Dreamers, Noora's Quest* was published in March 2022.

Visit R.Y. Suben website: https://ryucebay.wixsite.com/rysuben

Aim your camera's phone at the QR code.

Follow R.Y.:
Blog: https://rysuben.com/
Instagram: https://www.instagram.com/writing4children/
Twitter: https://twitter.com/suben_r

Made in the USA
Monee, IL
06 November 2022

17236030R00059